# The Family Curse

# The Family Curse

Inspired by a True Story

Derek & Tyronza Waithe

J. Kenkade
PUBLISHING®

LITTLE ROCK, ARKANSAS

The Family Curse
Copyright © 2021 by Derek and Tyronza Waithe

J. Kenkade Publishing
6104 Forbing Rd
Little Rock, AR 72209
www.jkenkadepublishing.com
Facebook.com/jkenkadepublishing

J. Kenkade Publishing is a registered trademark.

Printed in the United States of America
ISBN 978-1-955186-14-8

# *Dedication*

This book is dedicated to My Heavenly Father; Lord and Savior, Jesus Christ, who has given me these stories. To my grandparents (RIP), to my parents, my children, my brothers, sisters and all the Royal Family that are locked down or free, and all those that are resting in peace.

To family and friends,
you know who you are,
Royal Love.

Special thanks to the women who gave me seven reasons to love. Thanks for my children. Special thanks to Dwight and Maudie Gamble, love you both.

To all of those locked down in the Federal
and State prisons; keep your heads up.

REST IN PEACE
TO MY ANGEL GRANDDAUGHTER
Brynlee Yvette Waithe
Papa loves you!

# Table of Contents

# INTRODUCTION

The Family Curse is a novel that will open your eyes to two words, FAMILY and Curse. There are many families in the world that do not know why they are having the problems that they are facing... I hope to open the eyes of the reader.

FAMILY: A group of people of common ancestry (Line of descent: Lineage; ancestor; to go before one from whom an individual is descended) (Generation: a body of living beings constituting a single step in the line of descent from an ancestor)

CURSE: Evil or misfortune coming as if in response to a CURSE!

Now a curse cannot come without a cause. Proverbs 26:2 says, "Like the sparrow in her wanderings, like the swallow in her flying, so the causeless curse does not alight.

Joshua 7:10-26. Tells a story of how a man brought a curse upon his family because of greed. But yes, the curse can be broken. Numbers 16:46-49. This is another story that shows us how we are to stand in the gap for the family to redeem them from a curse that has been caused by someone in our FAMILY.

So, we see that every cause has an effect.

Cause: Reason or motive; something that brings about a result; especially a person or thing that is the agent of bringing something about.

Effect: Result

Now that we have covered that, I would like to share with you something that one of my sons posted on facebook. I felt that it would be perfect for this novel to show the Cause and Effect of our actions.

10/20/19

## THE EFFECT!

When I was my momma's baby boy, I never pictured my life this way at 22! I lost my dad when I was 5 and no, he's not dead, but it's been plenty of nights it felt like it! My grandma raised me, and she lived with my great grandma. My great grandma Todd got sick when I was in the 5th grade. Me and my brothers spent every day with her even when she was healthy cause like I said, my grandma raised us. One night my mom came to pick us up. We all went and hugged Grandma Todd and told her we were leaving and that we loved her. My last words to my great grandma were, "I love you!" And then I kissed her. She died that same night. My mom woke me up out of my sleep and said we are going to Grandma Neal's house. We got in the car, and she looked and said, "You know why?" I looked and tears started to roll. I said, "Grandma Todd", just a boy in the 5th grade.

My mom married a man and I loved him like my father, and he loved me like his son. He moved his kids in with us and they became my brothers. We loved one another like we were twins. But they were young, and every boy needs his momma, so they went back to her.

I graduated high school and started Rend Lake College. One day my mom's husband asked me to take him to the courthouse. He got out and said, "Ight Tink." I got home from school and my stepdad wasn't there. He was going to sit down for a few years. My two older brothers had already moved out. It was just me and my 'lil' brother. He became my everything and he didn't even know it. He said he felt like I didn't love him and that kilt me.

Only a few knew I been through this, but I had to let it out because I told my baby's momma I was depressed and sad. She flipped out on me and said, "You sound stupid. You got everything! Boy you literally have everything you want and need to be content." P.S. This was while she was carrying my daughter. Then I lost my daughter and I swear my heart was getting colder. I be feeling like I don't need nobody, but myself! This **** ain't for likes. I just had to let this out. This **** made me the man I am today, and I came a long way!

## THE CAUSE!

Sitting in federal prison today like I have done for the past 17 plus years, there isn't a day that goes by that I don't think of my children, my parents, and my grandchildren. Also, I can't forget the woman who has loved me through all of this.... Tyronza our love is forever and will always be. I dedicate "Ain't No Woman Like the One I Got" by the Four Tops. I love you wifey.

But today as I read what my Junior said on Facebook, it made me reflect on all the years I have missed. I've missed my sons growing into the men that they have become, and I've missed seeing my baby girls become the women they are today...I haven't had the opportunity to witness the birth of any of my grandchildren or spent a birthday with my youngest son, Derrion. I haven't been able to go and sit, laugh, and make jokes with my mother or drive her across the country like I used to. Nor have I been able to just pop up on my pops... But reading this passage today also showed me how my actions caused my son to have to look at another man as a father figure. (I respect Vee though because he didn't have to.) But my actions caused that effect.

I think about the last time I got to speak to my grandma, and how I had to receive the news of her passing while I was here in prison. God had prepared me for her death a day before, but I wasn't prepared to talk with my mom that morning. When she got on the phone I broke down. It hurt because I couldn't be there for my favorite girl. I stood there crying tears of sorrow because I knew that my mom was trying to be strong for me. She was the one who had lost her mother...

My son just lost his daughter, and I can't begin to imagine how it feels. It hurt my soul as I stared at a picture of my granddaughter's dead body. I cried when I saw my son holding his only child's body and wasn't able to spend one day with her alive as I have done with mine...I spoke with his mother and told her I was sorry for causing her to carry this weight alone... If I could start my life all over again, I would do so many things differently! I would change my priorities to what I see now is important. My heart is heavy when I think about material things meaning much more to me than relationships. I would walk away from it all just to be there when my grandmother passed away and to stand beside my mom when she lost her husband. I would walk away to spend a birthday with Derrion and to hold Tink in my arms when his daughter passed. I would cherish the moments to have been there when Ja'Ron, Isaiah, Kingston, (aka King), Jaxson, and Aiyla (aka Queen) were born. I would be there for Tyronza during the passing of her grandmother. I realize now that there is NOTHING worth losing time with family and loved ones!

In case you haven't realized that your actions cause an effect in your family, I hope you have now! Enjoy this novel. It will open your eyes to many things that we as a people may not have known.

Thank You!

OPAL TOMETI
ALICIA GARZA
PATRISSE CULLORS
ARE THE REASON OUR VOICES
ARE BEING HEARD!

BLACK LIVES MATTER!
THANK YOU!

# Prologue

Jake cried crocodile tears as he cocked the Desert Eagle and pointed the weapon before firing. "Bang!"

At that very moment at the hospital, Dr. Taylor rushed into Little Jake's room with a medical team. Jake Jr. had flat lined. The beeping sound from the monitor rang out. Dr. Taylor began to do CPR as one of the nurses cut away Little Jake's gown. Another nurse produced a defibrillator. The CPR wasn't working. Doctor Taylor asked for the defibrillator paddles.

After the nurse charged the defibrillator, the doctor yelled out. "Clear! Now!" She shocked the child with the paddles. After each try, she did another round of CPR. Dr. Taylor tried and tried. She yelled out. "Come on baby, fight! You have to fight!" as she continued to apply CPR. Tears rolled down her face as one of the nurses grabbed her by the shoulder. Dr. Taylor dropped her head and shook it back and forth.

Dr. Taylor lifted her head and checked the time on the clock and said, "The time of death is 12:55 PM," as she swallowed the lump in her throat. The nurse recorded the time of Jake Junior's death.

Jacinta screamed out, "No Lord no! You said that everything was going to be alright, but you still took my baby away from me." She cried as she pressed herself against the glass and stared at her only child's lifeless body lying there.

Dr. Taylor held Jacinta and tried to comfort her as best as she could, but deep down inside she knew there was nothing she could say or do. "I am so sorry, we tried everything that we could, but his chances were slim from the beginning." Dr. Taylor said, holding back her emotions.

## JOY

JOY: A FEELING OF HAPPINESS THAT COMES FROM SUCCESS, GOOD FORTUNE, OR A SENSE OF WELL BEING. A SOURCE OF HAPPINESS, BLISS, DELIGHT, ENJOYMENT.

# CHAPTER ONE

I will never forget September 7, 2020. That was the day that changed my life forever. The sun was shining bright, birds were chirping and there was a nice breeze. The temperature was in the high seventies. I laid in bed thinking about how great my life was. I had everything I could dream of. I had a beautiful wife, who had birthed me a son. I couldn't ask for anything more.

The sun seemed to have been super bright that day. It shinned through the large window of our master suite, right on to the bed where I laid. I laid in the bed and looked at the many pictures that were displayed on the walls. I smiled as I looked at the large black and white picture of my wife and son a few days after his birth. But all that was interrupted when my son rushed into my room.

The double doors to the master suite burst open, "Daddy, wake up!" Little Jake age five, blurted out as he ran across the oak hardwood floors. He made his way towards his father who was acting as if he was asleep. Little Jake dove on top of his father who laid in a king size mahogany bed. "Daddy, wake up!" Today is the day that all the fathers come to school with their child. Now wake up!" Little Jake shook his father trying to wake him.

"Boy! What do you want? Don't you see me trying to sleep? It's only...." Big Jake picked up his phone off the nightstand to check the time... "it's seven-fifteen in the morning." Big Jake was twenty-nine years old. He stood five feet ten inches and weighed two hundred and fifteen pounds. He was brown skinned with wavy hair that connected to his beard and goatee. Big Jake was a ladies' man. He was very handsome. He looked at his son out of the corner of his eye as he pretended to fall back asleep. He loved his son more than anything and had cleared that entire day just to spend with his son.

"Daddy, you promised that you were going to come to my school today. So, get up!" He laid on top of his dad, dressed in his school uniform, black slacks, a white button-down shirt, a blue jacket with his school crest, and black shoes.

Big Jake opened his eyes and stare at his baby boy with brown skin and wavy hair. Little Jake's big brown eyes stared back, and big Jake always gave in to them. He was the joy of his life. Big Jake thought to himself just how much his son resembled his mother. "Little man I'm sorry but daddy can't make it today. Daddy's got some especially important business he needs to handle. You do understand, don't' you little man?" Disappointment surfaced on Little Jake's face. He climbed down out of the bed, dropped his head, turned around, and began to walk away. "Yes sir, I understand."

Little Jake said sadly as his eyes began to tear up.

"I got you! Daddy wouldn't miss this day for anything in the world." Big Jake smiled and said, "Who is the greatest dad?"

Little Jake turned back around and ran towards his father who held his arms open for a hug. "You are daddy! You're the greatest dad in the whole wide world!" Little Jake said as he jumped into his father's arms and gave him a kiss.

"And guess What?"

"What's that dad?"

"After school we'll spend the rest of the day together. Just us men. No mommy. Just you and me doing men things."

"No uncle Shanon or Uncle Mike either?"

"Nope. Just us." Big Jake stated as he gave his little junior a kiss.

"Alright daddy, I love you."

"I love you more son."

"Bye bye daddy. See you later." Little Jake yelled out as he ran out of the room and down the long hallway. The long hallway had more pictures of the family displayed on the wall. Many of them were baby pictures of little Jake, and family portraits. Big Jake laid in bed with a big smile on his face. He could hear his son singing as he ran across the white marble floors.

"My daddy is coming to school today with me." He repeated that phrase over and over again.

Big Jake just shook his head and smiled knowing that little Jake was about to run into a big problem and get in trouble for running in the house. Little

Jake made his way to his mother who stood in the foyer of the 5000 square foot brick home that was located on the far west side of Joliet IL. She stood there waiting on him to take him to school. She heard his little song and the pats of his running feet.

Jacinta, stood near a spiral staircase and yelled to little Jake. "Boy, I've already told you once this morning to stop running in my house! You're going to keep on trying me till I pop you on your butt. Keep on." Jacinta was 26 years old stood five feet 7 inches and weighed one hundred and thirty-five pounds. Before becoming an accountant and bookkeeper for a small business, she was a runway model. Being half African- American and half Asian gave her a skin tone of a buckskin brown hue. Light green eyes, full lips, and a small beauty mark on her cheek contributed to her beauty. She had long black silky hair brushed back into a braided ponytail that reached down to the middle of her back.

She was dressed in a two-piece black pantsuit, gray silk blouse, and six-inch black, red bottom heels. Jacinta glanced at her son through the lenses of slim black Gucci framed eyeglasses as he ran towards her. She knew that he was overwhelmed with joy about the time he and his father were going to spend together. It also made her happy because she didn't want to see her baby disappointed and sad if his father would have let him down. But for weeks she had been on top of big Jake to make sure he could make it. Being a mother and black mother at that, she had to hate just the little bit.

"Boy get out of my face. I don't care about your daddy going to your school with you today. It's about time he did something. Now go get in the car." Jacinta said as she pointed her finger toward the car. Once Little Jake's back was to her, she smiled enormously as she watched him skip off and said to herself, "That kid is crazy about that man."

Little Jake stopped and turned around to face his mother and said, "Mommy my daddy said that me and him and nobody else were going to spend all day together after I get out of school." He turned back around and began to sing his song once again as he skipped away.

Jacinta stood there with a look on her face that said, "I know he didn't?" She then turned around towards the hallway and yelled out, "I don't care about you or your dad. I hope you two stay gone and never come back. Maybe then I can get some peace and quiet around here." While waving her finger in the air like she was talking in a sassy manner. Her left ring finger displayed a ten- karat diamond that sat atop a platinum wedding band. Her feelings had been scarred a little because she had been left out of the event.

"Lord forgive me for that lie. I love and care for my family. But Lord, that man knows how to get under my skin and work my nerves. Please Lord, give me strength to keep me from busting his head," she said as she looked up and repented. She turned around and grabbed her purse, briefcase, and her keys out of a crystal bowl that sat in the middle of a large cherrywood circular styled table. The table had been placed in the middle of the foyer under a crystal chandelier. "Get in your dad's truck! I'll show him. I'm going to burn all the gas out since I can't go with y'all." Jacinta said, as she walked out of the house. Big Jake rolled over and laughed. He had heard every word and knew she wasn't playing and in her feelings. He simply turned back over and went to sleep.

Jacinta got into the truck, looked over at her baby for a moment, then leaned over and gave him a kiss. "I am so sorry for saying I don't care about you and your dad. I love you both more than I love myself." She smiled. Little Jake smiled back as the oak garage door to the third bay opened. The sunlight penetrated the windshield of the new Range Rover and showered its dark gray leather with black piping seats. The sunrays hit and then glittered off the black and chrome rims. The natural light caused the transitional lens of Jacinta's eye glassed to turn a light maroon tint. As they pulled out of the garage, little Jake programmed his phone to tune into the truck's system and played the latest hit by T- Vegas of the Royal Family Cut- Throat. T-Vegas is Big Jake's little cousin. He'd gotten out of the federal penitentiary after doing 16 years of a forty-year sentence. The Fair Sentencing Act, under the Obama administration, changed laws that reduced harsh drug sentences. Not only him, but many other family members as well. Once they were all out, they dropped an album talking about their conspiracy.

As Jacinta pulled out of the garage and made it to the end of the driveway, she blew the horn and waved at a young white woman who was jogging by. Making a right turn out of the driveway, they rode through their community passing all the other large, beautiful homes.

Little Jake stared out of the window at some of the other kids that were standing on the corner laughing and talking while waiting on their school bus. Turning to his mother as they pulled up to the gate of their gated community little Jake asked, "Mommy?"

"Yes baby?"

"Why can't I ride the bus to school like my friends?"

"Because baby, I work so close to your school. Plus, I love driving you every day." She smiled as she looked at him and blew him a kiss. Jacinta pulled out of the gate, smiled, and waved to the young black security guard sitting in the booth. As she made a right turn on to Black Road, they enjoyed the music for a quarter of a mile before they came to the intersection of Black Road and Richmond Avenue. Jacinta was stopped by a red light. She put on her left turn signal and pulled into the left lane.

As they listened to the music, waiting for the light to change, Little Jake blurted out over the music and said, "Mommy."

"What is it baby?" Jacinta asked and looked over at her son. Little Jake had his dad's shades on and was trying to lean the way he'd seen his father do. He was so elated about the day. She could do nothing but laugh at him and shake her head.

"When I grow up, I am going to work where my daddy works because he always has a lot of money to buy us whatever we want." Little Jake stared back at his mother awaiting a response. Much to his surprise, she snapped!

"Oh no you're not! "You're going to be a doctor or lawyer, nothing like your dad!" Jacinta looked at her son with the most serious face she could. Little Jake didn't have any idea of who his father was. Part of his father was a very high-profile person in the underworld. He was the reason for so many other families' pain from the loss of their loved ones. That is the real reason why Jacinta takes Little Jake to school every morning and picks him up. "Now sit back and put your seat belt on." Little Jake looked over at his mother as if she'd lost her mind. He wondered what that was all about?

Little Jake went back to bounce his head and sing along with the music. He watched as two dogs ran and played in the park. As he looked on, he was surprised when a man in a black hoodie with a gun in his hand ran up. Seconds later shots rang out. Bang! Bang! Bang!

Jacinta screamed out "Jake!" as she dived from the driver's seat and on top of her child. She laid on top of him using her body as a human shield. Little Jake slumped down into the seat in a lifeless state. His white shirt turned red from his blood.

In the course, Jacinta was also hit with bullets. One entered her left leg while another pierced her left shoulder. Once the shooting ended, she felt the truck began to roll. It glided across Richmond Ave and hit a telephone pole. The horn sounded and the airbag deployed. The aftermath of the crash left the right fender jammed against the right front wheel causing the tire to blow out.

Once Jacinta knew that the shooting was over with for good, she reached into her purse and pulled out a small caliber handgun and looked up to see if she saw anyone. The OnStar operator came across the speaker. "Hello, this is your OnStar operator. My name is Janet. My system is showing this vehicle has been involved in an accident. Is everything alright?"

Jacinta screamed out, "No! Help me! Please send help! My son and I have been shot!" Jacinta applied pressure to Little Jake's wounds. Blood was flowing out from both of them like a faucet.

"Ma'am. Is the shooter still there?"

"No. I don't see anyone. Please hurry and send help!" Jacinta yelled.

"Alright ma'am. We are locked in on your location and help will be there shortly. I will stay on the line with you until help arrives." The operator said as she continued typing on the keyboard of her computer to the Joliet City Police Department and emergency workers.

"Ma'am, how are you doing? Can you tell me where you and your son were shot?" The operator needed all the information she could get in order to pass it on to the emergency crew so they could be abreast of the situation upon arrival. "Ma'am are you still there?" the operator asked with great concern.

"Yes, I don't know about my son, but I was hit in the left leg and left shoulder. Please Lord don't let my baby die!" Jacinta cried out to the Lord in pain about her child. She was unable to truly feel the pain from her own shots due to the pain in her heart as a mother when she's helpless and cannot do anything for her child. Jacinta held little Jake's limp body in her arms as tears rolled down her face. After two minutes of waiting, she heard the sound of nearing sirens.

"Ma'am, we have tried contacting the number that's listed for emergency on this vehicle, but no one is answering." The operator commented with tears in her eyes being a mother of two children herself. She seconded that emotion after hearing Jacinta cry out to the Lord over her wounded child.

"Don't worry about it. Thanks for everything. The police are pulling up right now." Jacinta ended the conversation. She stuck her gun back into her purse and picked up her phone and texted her husband. Then she called his phone. It was to no avail.

# CHAPTER TWO

"GO! GO! GO!" A man dressed in all black yelled as he jumped inside the vehicle from the passenger side. Once inside, breathing hard, he looked around to make sure there were no witnesses. As soon as everything seemed to be clear, he fell back into his seat, still breathing hard.

The driver threw the car in gear and asked nervously, "Did you get him? Is Jake dead?" He gripped the steering wheel tightly as he sped pass and saw Jake's Range Rover crashed into a telephone pole.

The driver watched as the passenger wiped down the gun before tossing it out of the window, as they crossed the bridge to the east side of town. Then he asked again. "So, is he dead or what?" He waited anxiously for a response. Beads of sweat formed on his forehead. His partner threw his hoodie back and let out a loud sigh.

The vehicle filled with silence momentarily, it seemed like a lifetime. All you could hear was breathing. He asked again but with a more commanding tone. "Fam, is he dead or what? Tell me something. Is Jake going to be a problem or what?"

"No." He said in a low tone then laid his back against the seat.

Shakily, he asked, "What was that?" eyes bucked. His hands began to sweat. "Did I hear you right? Did you say, No?"

"NO! NO! NO!" He yelled out as he slammed his fist against the dashboard. Fueled with anger, a vein popped in the middle of his forehead. Eyes red as fire, he said, "Jake has to be the luckiest nigga in the world."

Once again, the vehicle is filled with silence. Neither man spoke a word for miles. They didn't know what they were going to do if Jake found out they were the ones behind the attack.

The silence was broken. "If Jake's not dead, how did he get away? I heard the shots and I saw the truck. Did he get out and run?" He paused for a minute then asked, "Did he notice it was you? Don't just sit quietly over there, say something! You've got me over here in the blind. Because if he recognized you, he knows we're together all the time. If so, you know Jake is about to snap!" Fear was expressed with every word.

"He's going to do more than that!"

"What do you mean by that?" He turned and stared towards him and said, "He must have noticed you." He then began to beat his palms against the steering wheel. "I knew this wasn't a good idea."

"Naw, he didn't see me because he wasn't the one in the truck."

"Who da hell did you shoot? Somebody had to be in that truck." He thought to himself, who would have been in Jake's truck? Then said, "Don't tell me it was somebody with a truck like his?"

Before answering, he rubbed his chin and said, "I only wish....it was his wife and son. Jake is not going to snap; he is going to turn this city upside down." He shook his head.

"Whoa! Hold up. Are you serious? You shot his wife and son? Fam, you really have lost your mind," he said as his chest heaved faster and faster. He pulled out a blunt, fired it up, and took along pull. "This is not good," he said as he exhaled the smoke. "Why would you do that? Why did you go through with it when you knew Jake wasn't in the truck? You know women and children are off limits, no matter what." His hand shook as he passed the blunt. "Jake is going to go crazy. He is going to kill us. Not just us but everybody that is connected to us if he finds out it was us. You know that, right?" he said with a blank look in his eyes as he stared forward.

"Hey! Calm down! He will never find out because they are dead and the only ones that know are in this car. That is, you and me. Do. I. Make. Myself. Clear!" He asked as he pulled out another gun from his waist.

The gun pointed at him and the threat that was made were the least of his worries. He would never let on to Jake that he knew anything. How could he without implicating himself. There would be no way to explain it. Jake would not believe any-thing he said. He knew that was a death sen-tence. He was more worried about his family. Jake would kill them and make him watch. A bullet to the head would be better than what Jake would do.

Jake is known for torturing anyone who dares to cross him in any kind of way. He has a way of making the person he is torturing beg to be put out of their misery. Jake had a guy buried alive who had agreed to testify against him. The man's family is still searching for him. But what they don't know is that he is close to them. Jake had his guys bury the man in the man's mother's rose garden. That is how cold-blooded Jake is. He doesn't care if he feels that you have crossed him in any way. You will pay and it doesn't matter who you are. He tortured one of his own soldiers who had stolen a half a brick of cocaine. He tied the man to a chair and placed his feet in boiling water and insisted that the rest of the crew watch.

"Fam, do me a favor and shoot me." He leaned forward and placed his head on the barrel. "Do you really think I would say anything to Jake? How in hell could I explain it, huh!" He pushed the gun away from his face. "But what I don't understand is why you killed them. You know that is not how we roll. We don't get down like that. That is a no, no," he said as they came to a complete stop in a driveway.

They both sat in silence as they thought about the problem that they created.

"Little man saw my face as I walked up to the truck. I had the gun raised when I noticed it wasn't Jake. Me and lil man were staring eye to eye. How could I explain that? Me walking up on the truck with my gun raised. Once his mother would go back and tell Jake what had happened, there would be no stopping, Jake. He would come with a vengeance," he said and sat back quietly and contemplated how they would handle this. Then out of nowhere it seemed like he had a revelation to solve their problem. He sat straight up and said, "We good. You know the first person he is going to blame?"

With eyebrows raised he said, "Tone. You are right. He is going to go after Tone."

"That is right," he said with a big smile spread across his face. "Problem solved." Then he laughed out loud.

TRAGEDY
TRAGEDY: A SERIOUS DRAMA WITH SOR-
ROWFUL OR DISASTROUS CONCLUSION:
A DISASTOROUS EVENT: CALAMITY;
ALSO, MISFORTUNE

YOU NEVER KNOW WHEN TRAGEDY WILL
COME TO YOUR FRONT DOOR.

# CHAPTER THREE

BOOM! DING DONG! BOOM BOOM! DING DONG! BOOM! The time was 8:10 a.m. when the commotion woke Jake from a sound sleep. He was furious because the banging and the doorbell wouldn't stop. Jake jumped out of bed and grabbed his silk robe from off a chair. Jake stomped down the hallway in a rage at the commotion. He yelled out, "stop ringing the door bell and banging on my door like you have lost your mind!" Jake walked up to the door and asked, "Who is it?!"

"It's me cuz! Hurry and open the door!" Jake recognized the voice of his cousin Shanon who also had Mike with him. Mike was Jake's right-hand man. The three men had all grown up together in the church and spent numerous nights over one another's house.

As Jake opened the door, both men rushed in with their weapons drawn. Jake looked at them both dumbfounded then stuck his head out of the door to see if any of his neighbors were watching. He closed the door and asked, "Man what's up?! You can't come out here like that. These white folks will call the people (referring to the police). What's going on anyway?" Jake asked.

"Cuz, who got your truck?" Shannon asked hoping Jacinta would walk out to see what was going on. Jake could see that something had Shanon worked up and could see fear in his eyes. Shanon wasn't easy to scare and there was a deep concerned look on his face.

Then Jake looked over at Mike, who was standing by the window with his AK47 in hand. Jake looked back at Shanon before he spoke and said, "Nobody has my truck. Why? What's up?" Jake asked, looking back and forth between the two men. Shannon was 29 years old, stood six feet five, and two-hundred and seventy-five pounds. He was dark skinned and wore a low haircut. Jake looked back at Mike who was also 29 years old. Mike was six feet even, two hundred and fifteen pounds and was high yellow with corn rows hanging down to his shoulder. Jake wondered why he kept staring out of the window. Still confused, Jake demanded. "Somebody needs to tell me something and I mean fast!"

"Cuz, are you sure your ride is here?"

"What?! What I say!" Jake insisted, then walked over to the door that led to the garage. But to his surprise, when he opened the door; he saw that Jacinta's white Cadillac Escalade and his dark blue Ferrari parked. Jake turned around with fear in his eyes. He knew something had gone terribly wrong. "What happened?" Jake insisted on knowing. Jacinta had taken little Jake to school in it. As he waited, he remembered her saying that she was going to drive out all his gas. With the most worried and angry face, he could muster up, he commanded, "Now tell me what happened?" Shanon dropped his head and Mike went and copped a seat on the chair. He rested his face in the palms of his hands and shook his head back and forth.

"Man, somebody shot up your truck at the corner of Black Rd and Richmond. It's been all over the news for the last hour. Cuz, your wife and little Jake were in that truck." Shannon said as he stared at his cousin. He could see the fear on Jake's face.

Jake shouted, "What?! No, no! Shot my wife and son?" Tears ran down Jake's face. He asked, "Man, are you sure?" still in shock.

"Yea cuz. I am sure it was your truck," Shanon said as he shook his head. "I called Mike so that he could meet me here to check on Jacinta and little man but when you came to the door, I didn't know what to think."

Jake stood there still in shock and thought about who could have waged war against his family. Jake always played by the rule, that whatever happens in the streets, stays in the streets. You never bring a man's family into it. That's just one of the codes of the streets.

"Jake, it has to be Tone. Remember that beef last month that went down over on the East side with a few of our guys and his? One of his got burned (killed) in the shootout." Mike said, as he looked up at Jake with anger in his eyes. Jake walked into the family room and turned on the 80-inch screen TV to channel 13 WCT news.

"Now an update on the shooting that happened around seven forty-five this morning. A woman and child were attacked at Black Rd and Richmond Ave. The authorities say they believe that the hit was meant for Mr. Jake Lamont Johnson, who is also known as Jay Jay Johnson, the boss of the infamous Hilltop Gangsters. He has been brought up on numerous charges in the past five years including two murders and an attempted murder charge. None of the charges were able to stick due to missing witnesses. Each of the charges eventually fell by the wayside. The witnesses all seemed to have disappeared from the face of the earth, according to the authorities.

He is also related to the multi-platinum rap group, Royal Family Cut-Throat, whose label is simply known as Royal family. The CEO, along with other artists on the label were sentenced to serve significant sentences in the federal prison system on a large drug conspiracy in southern Illinois. Changes due to the Fair Sentencing Act and the First Step Act, gave way to all the members receiving substantial reductions in their sentences, thus being released. Mr. Johnson is said to have money invested in the Royal family label as a scheme to clean up and laundry his street profits."

Jake stood and watched himself on the TV screen. Pictures of his family members were also being flashed across the screen. Jake picked up a bat and threw it into the TV screen. Then he ran out of the front room, down the hallway and into his bedroom. He picked up his cell phone to see that he had an unread text. The text read: "Baby, the baby and I are at Saint Joseph's hospital. Somebody walked up on the truck and shot into it from the passenger side where little Jake was sitting. Honey I don't know if he is going to make it or not. I need you to hurry and get here. I can't do this by myself. I can't take it alone. Please, I need you as soon as possible. I love you."

Jake fell to the floor and yelled out loudly. He cried with his face sunk deep into his hands, thinking of the plans he and Little Jake had for the day. Once Jake pulled himself together, he got up and walked over to the dresser, pulled open the top-drawer, and pulled out a Chrome Desert Eagle. He got dressed and summoned for Mike to come to the bedroom.

"Mike, let me holler at you." Jake said, as he watched Mike walk into the room. Mike noticed that Jake was dressed in an all-black sweat suit, black Tims, and had his gun in his hand.

Mike said, "Yea, what is it family? What you need me to do? Name it and it's done." As he stood in front of his childhood friend and looked him in the eyes. He could see the hurt traces in Jake's face. Mike hadn't seen this look since Jake lost his father.

Jake looked Mike straight in the eyes full of anger and rage. As the anger filled him, he said, "Go get Tone's old lady. She should be down at the salon she owns. It should be opening right about now. He wants to play games then we'll show him how the game is played. Take her to that spot we just copped in the hood. Call Pooh and have him dig a hole out in the woods someplace. Don't let him know who it is for and do that without hurting anyone else. We really don't need the extra heat right now. If I'm gonna lose one, he will lose two. JaRonda is pregnant."

Mike could tell that Jake was dead serious. With so much hate and anger built up at that point, Jake decided that he was not going to be the only hurt one, losing a family member. "Fam, I got this. Don't worry about anything. That's my family also. We're brothers. When you hurt, I hurt." Mike said as he looked Jake straight in the eyes. "You can count on it getting done."

Moments later after Jake and Mike were talking in the bedroom, Shanon called out for Jake. "Jay Jay, auntie is here." Jake and Mike looked at each other, finished up their conversation and walked up to the front of the house. Jake's mother was standing in the family room waiting. She had come to the house after getting the news about her grandson and daughter in law.

"Hey baby come here. I just saw the news, plus Jacinta's mother called me from the hospital." She said as she hugged her son tightly. "They are already up at the hospital with your family. She said your wife has been asking about you. Therefore, I came to take you up there. That is where you are needed the most. Let's go be with your family. Jacinta needs you right now. This is the time that you have to be strong, alright?" Mrs. Johnson knew her son and what they were planning. She knew Jake had other plans. What mother doesn't know her child? As she grabbed Jake's hand he fell to the floor on his knees. He had broken all the way down.

"Momma why? Why momma? My... my family? I would never do this to another man. I wouldn't bring a man's family into our problems. I don't know what I'll do if my son dies." Jake said as he rested his head against his mother and cried even harder.

Mrs. Johnson pulled her son up onto his feet. She placed her arms around him and assured him that everything will be alright. "Baby, I don't know what to say, but If you let God handle things, it'll turn out alright. God knows how to handle things the right way. There isn't a problem too hard for him to conquer. Believe me on this. You can't solve or fix this the way you want to. What if…" Before she could finish, Jake stepped back out of her arms.

"I'm not trying to hear this right now. There is no God! If there were a God, He wouldn't let stuff like this happen. You can keep all that God Bull Shhh." But before Jake could finish, he felt the sting of his mother's hand from the smack she applied to his face.

As she looked her son in the eyes, Mrs. Johnson said, "I know you dun lost your mind. I brought you into this world and I will take you out! You may frighten those guys out in those streets, and whoever, but you don't scare me. You're not going to disrespect me or My Lord! Do you understand me? Jake Lamont Johnson?" She asked with her finger pointed at him. Jake, Mike and Shanon all stood there in shock. Jake held the side of his face.

"Yes, ma'am. I do."

"Alright. The devil is a lie. You dun lost your mind talking to me like that." Then she continued to finish what she was saying. "Now as I was say-ing, what if something happens to you? Then I'll be without a son and a grandson. It's already hard for me at night knowing you are living your life the way you do. When the phone rings at night, I fear that it's a call saying that you're dead or something. Right now, it's my only grandson, my sunshine in the hospital fighting for his life. Baby please just walk away. Let God have control. By his son, Jesus Christ' stripes, he will heal Little Jay Jay, if you just walk away. Let God punish the one who is responsible." Mrs. Johnson grabbed her son by the hand and pulled him close to her to hug him. And said, "the Bishop is already at the hospital along with some of the mothers from the church. So, let's go and be with your family. Come on Shanon, you're going to drive us." Jake dried his eyes. Shanon walked out the house to his car. Jake walked over to Mike and whispered to still handle the business. Mrs. Johnson said to Mike, "Mike you be careful. Go and get your family and bring them up to the hospital. We all should be together because we need all the prayers and blessings we can get." Mrs. Johnson wanted to keep all the guys together. She knew that each one of them cared so much for the other that they would take care of business in the place of the other.

"Yes ma'am. I've already told Lisa to go up there to be with Jacinta. I will be there shortly." He said, as he leaned over and gave her a kiss.

"Alright Mike, I mean it! You better get there, or you will be getting smacked across your face when I see you." She gave Mike a look as to say, 'try me if you want to.'

They all walked out of the house. Jake walked over and opened the front door of Shanon's Jaguar.

Mrs. Johnson obliged her son and sat down on the tan leather interior. On the way out of the gated section of the community, Jake noticed a dark blue unmarked Crown Victoria parked right outside of the entrance. He knew who it was and why they were there. But he figured that when they saw his mother in the car, they would not follow or pull them over to question him. But he knew sooner or later the feds would be coming around to ask questions that they knew they wouldn't get the answer to.

In route to the hospital, Shanon had to drive the same way as Jacinta, when she was taking little Jake to school. As they rode, everybody in the car thought about having to come to the intersection where the shooting had taken place, but no one spoke. As they approached the intersection of Black Road and Richmond Ave, they could see glass still on the ground. Police officers were still at the scene. The spot where the shooting had taken place was taped off and one of the officers directed traffic away from the crime scene. Jake noticed that his Range Rover was placed on the back of the flatbed tow truck. The area where the SUV had struck the pole was also taped off. Jake stared at his truck and could only imagined what his family had gone through an hour earlier at that very location while he lay asleep at home. A feeling of guilt, disbelief, disappointment, and responsibility reigned upon him, knowing that he was the reason for it all.

"Baby, are you okay?" Mrs. Johnson asked as she turned around to face her son. Shanon looked at him through his rearview mirror.

"Yes, I'm cool." Jake turned his head from looking at the SUV and assured his mother and cousin. "I am okay. You don't have to worry about me."

Jake sat in the back seat and thought about when Jacinta told him that they were with child. He was extremely excited. Concerned for their safety, Jake went and bought a new house in one of the best districts. He could not wait for the child to be born. He didn't care if it was a boy or a girl. He was simply happy that he and Jacinta were going to be parents. He loved knowing that she was just as excited as he. He loved making his wife happy. Jacinta was the love of his life.

The night little Jake was born, Jake couldn't sit still. He paced back and forth. Mike and Shanon made fun of him. They had never seen him so nervous. His auntie Denise told them to leave Jake alone. His father-in-law told him that his dad had responded the same way the night he was born. He said it was like watching Jake's father all over again.

When Jake was able to hold his son for the first time, he smiled big and then tears of joy streamed down the side of his face. He remembered the promise that he had made to his son that night. Son your dad will always protect you and I will never leave you. You will always be able to count on me for anything. Now Jake felt like he had let his son down. Someone had tried to take his life. Jake looked to the sky and said, "This is how I know that you're not real. If you were real, how could you allow something like this happened to a 5-year-old child?"

# CHAPTER FOUR

Detective Wallace was interrupted from his work when his cell buzzed to alert that he had a text message. After reading the message, he could not believe what he had read so he returned a message and asked, "Are you sure?" Once he received confirmation he said, "OMG!" out loud with wide eyes and a surprised tone. He laid the phone down on top of his desk and took in the info. He leaned forward towards his partner who sat across from him and said, "You are not going to believe what I am about to tell you."

His partner, Detective Foulks, never raised her head to make eye contact but said, "Why tell me if you know that I am not going to believe it?" In a sarcastic tone and rolled her eyes. "You know some of us have work to do and cases to close."

"Oh, trust and believe you want to hear this," he said knowing that he was irritating her by not divulging the information.

Detective Foulks let out aloud sign as she dropped her head and smacked both hands on top of her desk. She raised her head and stared at him then said, "What? What? What is it?! What is so unbelievable" she said with 'air quotes' that I won't believe but you are so sure that I want to know?" With brows lifted

Before he could answer she said, "We have a Black Lives Matter movement going on in the streets of the city. There are thousands of people protesting for George Floyd a black man killed by a white cop who held his knew on Mr. Floyd's neck for 8 minutes and 46 seconds. He continued to for a minute and 23 seconds after life had left his body. The man was handcuffed and held face down on the ground.

Let's not forget Ms. Breonna Taylor who was also killed by another white cop who shot her in her home. They claimed that they were looking for her ex-boyfriend when they had already had him in custody.

We are black officers, and our very own people don't trust us. When they see us some of them are afraid and the other ones look at us crazy with hate in their eyes not knowing we are just as pissed as them. But we have a job to do and protect this city. We must keep the agitators and looters in control. We must make sure the businesses don't get looted and burned down. So, what is it?"

Det. Wallace sat quiet for a moment. He thought to himself, she can't be serious. Detective shook his head in disbelief and then said, "You don't have to tell me what is going on out there, or the reason behind protecting. I wish I could be out there with them. I would be on the front line. I am a black man in America in case you hadn't noticed. That could have been me, my son, my father, or my brothers. I am George Floyd!" he said with anger in his voice. I work here just like you. I work with the same racist people that you do. They think I am beneath them because of the color of my skin," he said as he pointed to the back of his hand. "Even though I out rank them.

You don't think I hate it when I see how a white officer threats a black man? Huh?! Because I do. But what really gets to me is when I see how we threaten our own people. We really show our behinds when there is a white officer on the scene. The black officer act like he has something to prove.

Plus 98% of the time the officer/officers will get off. There could be all the evidence needed but this so-called blue wall keeps them from getting convicted." Det. Wallace stopped speaking and breathed in to calm himself down. Then said sternly, "Don't you ever come at me like that again."

Det. Foulks could tell that he was upset and rightfully so. She knew she was wrong for going at him like she did and said, "I am sorry. I am just frustrated. So, again I apologize."

"It is all good and I know you are. I am too. But back to what I was saying. It's about the shooting. You know the one that happened this morning."

"What about it?" She asked.

"Guess who it was?"

Det. Foulks laughed to herself and shook her head. She shut her eyes and said, "I just told you that I was frustrated. I don't have time to play these guessing games with you. This is a police station not a game show. So, whatever it is, please spit it out."

Det. Wallace laughed and said, "Anyway, it is Jacinta Johnson. A.K.A. Mrs. Jake, 'Jay Jay' Johnson. His wife was the one shot." He shook his head up and down.

Det. Foulks couldn't believe what she had just heard from her partner. She was speechless. Det. Wallace couldn't believe what he was witnessing. The woman with the witty comebacks was speechless. This was a first.

Then she said, "I can't believe it."

"I told you that you wouldn't." he said with a smirk. "But that's not the worst part." His demeanor changed and Det. Foulks thought, what could be worse?

"What could be worse than a woman getting shot?" she asked with a puzzled look.

Det. Wallace exhaled and said, "Their son was shot also."

Det. Foulks gasped for air as she gripped her chest. She fell back into her chair and there was silence between them. She tried to wrap her head around the fact that a woman and a child were paying for the sins of the one who is supposed to protect them...

Det. Foulks has been trying to build a case on Jake for years, but he seems to always beat any charges brought against him.

"Do you know what this mean?" She asked.

"Yes." Then he fell back into his seat.

"It is about to get ugly out there in those streets. It's about to be a war zone. Jake is going to go crazy. Who would even dare to attack his family? They must know he would not stop until he finds out. And when he does," she shook her head. "There will be nothing to stop him. It's nothing anybody can do to help them. They just signed their own death certificate." She exhaled and said, "How are we going to control the protesting and this when Jake unleashes, hell upon the city? It is going to be a nightmare!"

The two of them sat there thinking to themselves. Neither of them knew how they were going to get ahead of this because Jake must know already. Jake may have already been on the attack. They know Jake has a way of doing things under the radar. So how would they catch him?

Det. Foulks thought that this would be the best opportunity to catch Jake slipping. She said aloud, "Jake is going to make a mistake. This is personal to him, and he will handle it himself." She seemed to have gotten excited and there was a twinkle in her eyes. "We are about to bring this slippery bastard down." She smiled an evil smile. "He is about to pay for everything he has gotten away with. His time has come back and knocking at his door. He will know how all the families feel that he has caused pain." She had a devilish look in her eyes.

Det. Foulks picked up the phone and made a call. After completing the call, she stood to her feet and said, "let's go to the hospital. Jake is there. Let's go and ask some questions and hope he says something that we can lock him up for the rest of his life."

I CAN'T BREATHE
IS WHAT WE ALL HEARD
GEORGE FLOYD (8:46)
ERIC GARNER
ERIC HARRIS
AND
JAVIER AMBLER
SAY. WHY COULDN'T
THEY?

# CHAPTER FIVE

Shanon pulled into the parking lot of Saint Joseph's Hospital at eight fifty-five. The ride took less than fifteen minutes from Jake's house. Once Shanon parked his car he reached over into the glove box and pulled out a 9-millimeter handgun. He looked his auntie in the face as she shook her head, but she knew the life that her son and nephew lived plus she hadn't always been saved. Jake stepped out of the vehicle first and scanned the perimeter for a moment. Shanon did the same. They checked for anything out of the ordinary. Living the lifestyle, they lived, they knew the shooter would try again even at the hospital, if he knew that he had missed his target.

"Alright auntie, it's cool." Shanon said as he continued observing the perimeter.

"Yea, I don't see anything either that we should be worried about." Jake said, as he walked back to the car and opened the door for his mother. Shanon looked over at Jake as he tucked the 9-millimeter in the waist of his pants. He used his shirt to shield it.

"Cuz, it is going to be alright. Don't worry. We've been through a lot together and made it through.

Plus, we have God on our side. Remember that it's nothing but church folks up there praying for Lil Jay Jay." Shanon said as they made their way into the hospital. Jake looked over at him with a look that said, "Man miss me with all that."

Jake walked in front of his mother while Shanon followed behind as they walked through the hospital doors. Jake started to feel extra nervous. They were greeted by a little white lady with a head full of white hair, seated behind the service counter. "Hello. How may I help you?" She asked with a big smile.

"Hello, can you direct us to the intensive care unit?" Mrs. Johnson asked as she smiled back at the woman.

"Yes, take the elevator to the third floor, go to the right, and you'll run right into it."

"Thank you ma'am." Mrs. Johnson said. They walked over to the elevator. Jake pressed the elevator button. He started to reflect on the last time he was inside this very same hospital. It was five years earlier when Jacinta gave birth to little Jake. That was the happiest time in Jake's entire life. Now he was here once again regarding his son. Only this time it was the most frightful Jake had been in his entire life. He could not remember a more sorrowful point in his life, besides the passing of his father.

The elevator doors opened and as they entered, Jake heard the music to an old church song playing. There were no words just instrumental. It seemed as if he was the only one that heard it. 'Turn it over to Jesus, he can work it out' was the old tune.

The doors opened and they followed the instructions that were given to them. As they walked down the hallway, Jake noticed that Bishop Walker and his wife were seated in the waiting area. Bishop Walker was reading the Bible. Jake also notices the mothers from the church were there. They were standing in a circle holding hands and praying. The closer they got they could hear the women praying in that spiritual heavenly language of tongues.

Jake walked into the waiting area and over to his in laws. He hugged and kissed his mother-in-law, auntie, and his father-in-law shook hands. His father-in-law stood to his feet and looked Jake square in the eyes. He asked, "How are you son? You know you must be strong for your wife right now. It has been hard on her. She's been waiting for you. She told me that she is afraid that you are going to lose it, go out and do something stupid. So, reassure her that you're not and that everything is going to be alright no matter what." Jake stood in front of his father-in-law whom he loved and respected. His father-in-law, still holding his hand with a look in his eye that said, 'this is not a suggestion this is an order.'

Jake then said with pure hatred in his voice. "No, I will not lie to her and tell her that. I can't. Whoever it is that's responsible for this pain that we are feeling right now is going to wish they never crossed me. I am going to make them feel the same pain but 100 times worse. I am going to kill their entire family and make them watch. If they have a dog, I am killing it too. So, I will not tell her that. You know the rules of the game. You try and take one of mine; I come and take one of yours. This is different. It's personal now. They came for my family instead of me. You're an O.G. and that is also your family in there too. You know the coded of the streets. Ain't nothing changed since you and my father ran them." Their conversation had gotten a little heated. Everybody in the waiting area focused on the two of them.

Jake's father-in-law spat back and said with just as much force. "Yeah, you're right. That is my family in there too. But let me tell you something son. You're my family also. I love you just as much as I love them. Your father and I did run those streets, but where is he now? He is dead. My best friend is dead. I lost my best friend to those same streets that you're in. We never meant for you, Mike, or Shanon to follow in our footsteps. We didn't sit around and talk about you guys being in the game. We wanted more for you all. We wanted you guys to become something. We put work in to give our children a better life. You guys have taken it to another level, and I don't know what to tell you. Yes, you're the boss. You picked up where we left off." Jake's father-in-law paused for a second to calm himself down then said, "But one thing I am going to say. I hope you don't cause my little baby girl to hurt the way your mother Ruby had to for years after your father's death." Jake knew that his father-in-law was saying nothing but the truth. He vividly remembered the pain his mother went through after his father's death. "So, from man to man, promised me that much," he asked before sitting back down beside his wife whose face was full of tears.

As he looked at his father-in-law, Jake said, "alright. I'll let her know. I love her too much to add anymore strain to her load right now." But deep down he knew that he wasn't going to. Jake looked over to his mother and everyone else before walking away to be with his wife.

Jacinta was sitting in a wheelchair. She was staring at her son through a window. Little Jake laid there with all kinds of tubes running through his tiny body. Jacinta saw Jake's reflection in the window as he walked up. He reached out and touched her on the shoulder.

"Hey sweetheart, what are the doctors saying?" He asked as he knelt at her side. He kissed her on the lips and asked. "Are you going to be, OK?" He wiped the tears from her face, but she cried even harder after he appeared and touched her. Jacinta was relieved that Jake was there with her.

"Baby I'm so glad you're here with me now. I was worried about you. I am going to be alright, but..." Jacinta paused, took a breath, and said, "I. I found out that I was pregnant, but we lost the baby." She tried to hold back more tears from coming. Jake stood there and couldn't believe what he was hearing. He had no idea that Jacinta was with child.

"When did you find this out?" Jake asked.

"I was six weeks. I was going to surprise you. I had started making plans to have a dinner with the family and was going to tell everybody at the same time." Jacinta started to cry even harder now. "The doctor said that he has only a 30% chance of making it. Can you believe that? We have lost our unborn child and now we may lose little Jake." Jacinta said in between cries as she rested her head against Jake. "Baby they shot him three times in his little chest with a 38. The doctor said he is lucky to still be alive. One of the bullets missed his heart by a centimeter."

Jake felt the rage boiling inside of him and is glad that Jacinta hasn't said anything about him letting it go. He didn't want to make a promise that he knew he wasn't going to keep. Then he heard something come from her that he never imagined she would ask him. "Jake, I want you to promise me that you will not take it easy on the person or persons who is responsible for this. I want them to hurt and hurt bad. I want you to make them suffer. If little Jake doesn't make it, I want you to make them watch as someone they love die. If I must watch my child die, they need to watch their love one die." Jacinta said to Jake as she looked at his reflection through the window. A single tear rolled down the side of Jake's face as he stared back.

"That is a promise you don't have to worry about. I am already on top of it. I have an idea who may be behind this."

"Who is it?" Jacinta asked with anger in her voice.

"Tone."

Jacinta sat quietly for a moment and then said. "I want to be there. Get him somewhere and call me. I want to be the one who pulls the trigger."

"Whatever you want, my love." Jake said with no doubt that she would not be down for putting in the work. Jake kissed his wife and went back to looking at their critically hurt child. Jake was happy that he had the Ok from his wife because he knew that he was never going to let the situation go. Someone had to pay.

Time had passed. Jake and Jacinta sat patiently waiting for a change of their child's condition when Bishop Walker entered the ICU and asked Jake. "Brother Jake, I need a moment of your time. Jake turned around to face Bishop Walker, nodded to him, kissed his wife, and walked out behind Bishop Walker.

"Sir what is it?" Jake asked as they shook hands.

"You know I love you as if you were my own son. Your father, Jacinta's father, and I all ran the streets together. After years of running the streets, I chose to go another route and leave the game behind. That's when I took this path. I have never stopped loving them. We all remained good friends. But you know that. They respected my calling, and I respected their choices. I tried my hardest to get them to walk away from the game like I did. A week before your father's death; he came to my house to pick you up. We had a long talk. He said to me that if there ever came a time that he was unable to be there, for me to let you know that he always came to me for advice before reacting to a situation. Sometimes he listened and sometimes he didn't. Your father was a very head strong man, much like yourself." Bishop Walker said and then walked over to make him and Jake a cup of coffee. He pointed to a table where they could sit and talk.

"There is something I know you don't know. The night your father was murdered he called me about a situation where two and a half million dollars came up missing. I said that he should walk away. I told him I had been praying for him and Joe. And God told me to tell him that if he doesn't walk away, his actions would bring his wife much pain for years to come. His actions would not only affect her, but his sister Denise as well. He loved his baby sister to death. She was his only family besides Ruby, you, me, and Joe. Like I said, he was very head strong. The man had too much pride to just let anything go. It wasn't like he needed the money. He had more than enough. He had plenty. Your dad had to prove that he was not weak. Everybody knew that already. Regrettably, his pride was powerful, and it controlled him.

Joe would have been there with your father. They didn't make a move without one another. However, that day your dad told Joe that he was going to let it go. That he had talked to me and was going to take my advice. So that is the only reason Joe is still with us, by the grace of God. For many years Joe wished he had been there with your father. He believed that there would have been a better outcome, or they would have died together. They were awfully close. But it wasn't in God's plan, not saying your father's death was either." Bishop Walker could see a strange look on Jake's face when he said that. "Your dad didn't take heed to the warning. I believe your father would have been a great man of God. People respected him and knew how he lived his life. So, for him to have changed, many people would have followed him. I know I would have if he had walked away from the game before me.

Jake, when your father didn't walk away, he brought a curse on you and Shanon. God said that Ruby and Denise were going to have pain for many years because of his actions. See you and Shanon would continue to follow in the footsteps of your father. Even though my son Mike is a part of your crew, God has given me peace. He must live his life and suffer the consequences. I pray for you guys every day and night. I pray that something would cause you guys to walk away from the streets like I did.

Jake, God told me to tell you that he will heal your son, but you must walk away from this and let him handle it. What you have in store will not make peace within you. The only thing it is going to do is cause more pain for your mother and separate you and Jacinta. She may feel satisfaction once you get revenge, but it will only be temporary. She will start to blame you for the death of little Jay Jay. I know you do not believe in God, but just trust in me and believe what I am telling you about your dad. God wants to show you who he is and that his word will not come back to him void. Don't let the devil trick you out of your family and cause your mother and your aunt Denise to suffer any more pain." Bishop Walker stood to his feet and said, "You and Jacinta are making the wrong decisions. This is a Rhema word from God. I have no idea what you and your wife have talked about. I wasn't there and you haven't said a word since we talked outside of the ICU. So, think on that son." Bishop Walker said, as he patted Jake on the shoulder and walked away.

Jake sat there for a moment and thought about the conversation. It had him shook for a second. Jake made another cup of coffee and walked back into the ICU unit to where Jacinta was and handed her the coffee. She could see that Jake had something on his mind. She asked him what was wrong. Jake told her everything from his father's situation to what Bishop Walker said about their decision. He told her that he had never said a word about anything.

Jacinta, who is a believer, said to her husband, "If Bishop said all that then we will listen to him and let it go. Whatever you have in motion cancel it. I want my baby and I want my family. So, Jake, called it off." Jake just listened and patted Jacinta on the shoulder as to say, he agreed. Jacinta breathed a sigh of relief as she thought about Little Jake pulling through.

YOUNG BLACK MAN,
GONE TOO SOON!!

I AM
TRAYVON MARTIN!

# CHAPTER SIX

Forty-five minutes after leaving Jake's house, Mike was parked across the street from JaRonda's hair salon that was located on South Chicago St. He sat low in the seat of his Lexus talking on the phone. He checked the time and it read, 9:20 a.m. He wondered what was taking JaRonda so long.

Ten more minutes passed before he noticed her. JaRonda was in a red Mercedes coupe. Mike jumped out of his car and walked up to the driver's side and tapped on the window with the Chrome 380. JaRonda looked up to see Mike and screamed. He demanded that she open the door. She did as she was told. Mike took her by the arm and pulled her out of the car and told her to be quiet or he would shoot her in her pregnant belly. Mike walked JaRonda over to his car and opened the passenger door. He pushed her inside. He then walked around to the driver's side with his gun still pointed at her. JaRhonda sat very still. She held her large Chanel purse over her stomach as to protect her unborn child.

Mike looked at her and said, "Don't make this a homicide by trying something stupid. Do you hear me?" He asked, with a gun pointed at her head. JaRonda complied with a nod. She sat back in the seat, afraid for her and her unborn baby's life. Mike sped away from in front of her place of business. JaRonda had known Mike for years and knew exactly what he was capable of.

In route to the trap, Mike called Pooh. As the call was being made, he checked JaRonda out. JaRhonda had on some sandals that displayed her well manicure toes. The dress she had on permitted you to see her well-shaped chocolate tone legs. The pregnancy seemed to give her a glow. Her breast set up perfect. Her full lips were covered with a dark colored lipstick. JaRonda's long box braids were pulled up and none of her beauty was hidden. Mike thought to himself. "Man, I might have to have me some fun with this before I have to knock her brains back," as he licked his lips.

The ringing of the phone that sounded in his ear was replaced with Pooh saying, "What's up?"

"Pooh listen and listen closely. I need you to go and dig a hole out in the woods for me. And don't take anybody with you. Do this by yourself. You got it?" Mike asked as he looked over at JaRonda, who shivered with fright as she listened to Mike's conversation. She knew that the makeshift grave was for her. Mike gave her a smirk, as tears rolled down her face.

They rode for fifteen minutes before Mike pulled up to the house where Jake had ordered him to go. This spot was one of many that they did a lot of business, such as packing and distributing narcotics. Mike got out and open the door once again for JoRonda who noticed that there was plenty of wooded areas around. She thought to herself, where was her makeshift grave? Where would her body and her unborn child be buried. Her family will never be able to give her a proper burial. Mike pulled JaRonda by the arm, walked her inside the house, and pointed to the living room. He then walked into the kitchen and back out, moments later, with a glass of water. And handed it to her. He went back into the kitchen and called Pooh. Once Pooh answered, Mike asked, "Hey did you handle that yet?"

"Yeah, it's done. I took care of the hole."

"Alright, come through. I am at the spot, on Arthur Ave. Make sure you come alone and come right now." Mike had the cell on speaker and JaRonda could hear everything that was being said. Mike ended the call, walked back into the living room, and sat down in a chair across from JaRonda. Mike looked at her with an evil stare. She wondered why he had taken her hostage. She knew the code of the streets.

JaRonda asked. "What's the problem Mike? Why do you have me here? I have never done anything to you" with tears in her eyes holding her stomach. JaRonda was seven months pregnant at the time.

Mike stared back with evil in his eyes and his weapon on his lap and said, "Nah, you haven't done anything to me." Then he paused and bit down on his bottom lip and said, "but your man did. He crossed the line. He shot or either had someone shoot a woman and a young child today." He gave her a wicked smirk and said, "take a wild guess whose family it was?" JaRonda could only see pure hatred in Mike's eyes. Then he said to her, "I should just kill you for the fun of it," as he pointed his weapon.

"I think you're making a mistake. I don't know how you could think that Tone would do such a thing." Her eyes widened as she set up straight and said, "he couldn't have. We've been gone out of the country for the last two weeks. Plus, he would never do anything like that or have it done. Try and kill a woman and her child? That's not Tone. Jacinta's son is in our daughter Ke' Andra's class. Please call Jay Jay and let me speak with him. I can clear this up." JaRonda begged Mike to make the call because she could feel the magnitude of the situation.

Jake and Tone's beef goes back many years. All the way back to high school. Both started hustling weed in school and always tried to outdo the other. Once they got older and stepped their hustle game up, they have been beefing over whose crew would sell their drugs in certain neighborhoods. With all their beef, Tone moved his family out of harm's way, by moving them thirty miles outside of Joliet. JaRonda had been warned by Tone to only drop off their child at school, go to work, and then straight back out to where they lived and nowhere else. JaRonda knew all about Jake. He was well known for making people disappear. Jake was for sure nothing to be toyed with. The only other person around like Jake was her very own husband.

A knock came at the door. Mike yelled out, "who is it?!" as he walked towards the door.

"It's me." Pooh said, back from the other side of the door.

Mike let him in, and they headed straight for the kitchen. Pooh noticed JaRonda sitting in the living room as he walked past.

"Man, ain't that Tone's ole lady in there? What's up with that? You 'hit' that?" Pooh asked as he looked back at Mike.

"Nah.... but I just might tap that." Mike said enough for JaRonda to hear.

"Oh! Snap! Is that who the hole is for?" Pooh asked. JaRonda could hear everything said as she sat on the loveseat crying frantically. She could not help but think of how the choice of falling in love with Tone had brought her to this moment in her life. She knew everything about him before she even started dating him. But Tone was such a sweet person and always treated her with much love. He never laid a hand on her or even raise his voice in rage. There was nothing in the world he wouldn't do for her or their child. Tone never brought his street life to his home so she knew in her heart that he wouldn't have had anything to do with this. But now she will have to pay with her life for the life he led. His actions in the street had finally caught up with him and had reached his front door. Only if she would have never made the choice to date a guy that lived his life in the streets. She wouldn't be in this predicament.

"Jay Jay thinks that Tone had something to do with what happened this morning." Mike said as he looked Pooh straight in the eyes. "Who else could it have been? We're not beef'n with anyone else. Nobody else has the balls to step up to us. Go and put the guys on code blue. Tell them to make sure they are on point."

"Alright, but what about the new shipment we just got? You want us to hold out on moving it?"

"Nah, push it. This right here is just a small problem. It will be handled real soon. I am just waiting on the green light. I don't think little man is going to make it. And she won't either." Mike said, nodding towards JaRonda.

Pooh stood up and shook his head in disbelief. Then he walked out of the kitchen back past JaRonda. He stopped and looked at her and said, "I'd hate to be you right now. Man, what a waste. You're one beautiful but dead woman." He shook his head and yelled out. "Alright fam, count it as done." Then he walked out of the door.

Mike locked the door behind him. He walked back to the living room. JaRonda began to plead for her life and the life of her unborn child. But Mike wasn't trying to hear anything she had to say. He pulled out his phone and started to text. Seconds later he received one back. Mike looked up from reading the text and held the phone up so JaRonda could read the message. "Bruh, they said that my little man has only a 30% chance of making it. And if he doesn't make it, you know what that means. Better yet, I got something else in store for ole girl. She and dude are going to watch as their daughter takes her last breath. I got someone on the inside that works at the school who will snatch theirs once I send the word.

Then he is going to watch as she takes hers." JaRonda couldn't believe what she was hearing. Her body began to shake out of control. Jake was more wicked than she had heard. How could someone even allow those thoughts to enter their head. How could you premeditate about killing a five-year-old child who is innocent? The child had nothing to do with anything but will have to pay for the sins of the father. Regretfully, not just one but two. The unborn child would never be able to enter this world to have a chance to choose how he or she would live life. JaRonda started to pray out loud hoping that Mike would have some compassion on her. She asked God to forgive her for all her mistakes and to show Jake the truth.

Mike watched her and listened to her plea to God as he rolled a blunt and said, "God ain't gonna help you out of this. If there was a God, you wouldn't even be in this situation. But if there is a God, he has already shown Jake the truth. An eye for an eye!" Then he laughed loudly and hit the blunt. "You're dead."

"Mike how can you not believe that there is a God? Your father is one of the well-known preachers in the city. He has one of the largest churches. How can you not believe?" JaRonda asked. She was no longer crying. She was all cried out and had come to peace with her faith. She knew that Tone would make sure their daughter was protected once he discovered she was missing. Tone always checked on his wife to make sure she made it to drop their daughter off at school and that she made it to work.

Mike looked back at her, hit the blunt once again, stood up, and walked over towards her. He bent down and blew the smoke into her face and said, "if there was a God, he wouldn't allow me to be so cold hearted. If it is, he made me this way. Now shut up!"

JaRonda sat quietly and didn't say another word. She had just seen Satan face to face. Mike had so much hatred in him. She could feel it every time he stepped into the room.

SAY HER NAME!

BREONNA TAYLOR

BREONNA TAYLOR

BREONNA TAYLOR

BREONNA TAYLOR

BREONNA TAYLOR

# CHAPTER SEVEN

As Tone laid in the bed asleep, he was awakened by the ringing of his cell phone. He took a deep breath before answering. Once he noticed who was calling, he answered. "Hello." The caller on the other end started to explain something that seem to have Tone pissed off. "How did that happen?! How did you miss?! I thought you said you could handle it. Now it's going to be a big problem. Are you ready for this?! Are you ready for what is about to go down?! Uh? I'm asking you a question!" Tone snapped on the person on the other end of the phone. As the caller continued to explain to him, Tone reached for the remote and turn the on the TV. While flipping through the channels to the local news, he came upon a female news reporter who was covering the earlier stories. As Tone lay there listening to the news, he no longer focused on what the caller was saying on the line. He popped up and sat on the bed and said… "Let me get back to you." Tone ended the call. He listened to the news some more and watched as the news replayed footage from earlier. Tone thought of JaRonda. He picked his cell phone up again and spoke into the phone and said, "Call baby." JaRonda's cell rang but there was no answer. He immediately pulled up the shop number and called. The same outcome, no answer. Worry began to set in after trying to call JaRonda multiple times. Tone jumped out of bed and dressed as fast as he could. He opened the safe and pulled out a large black handgun, picked up his keys, and ran out of the house.

The ride back to the city of Joliet from Country Club Hills, takes 45 minutes straight down Interstate 80. Tone continued to call JaRonda and the shop but to no avail. His worry swiftly escalated to fear.

Tone exited the interstate onto Chicago Street and rode for two more miles before he came to a complete stop in font of JaRonda's salon. Tone felt some relief once he noticed her car parked in the salon parking lot in her very own personal spot. He exhaled and just thought that she was super busy and couldn't get to the phone. Tone grabbed his gun and tucked it into his waist, before he stepped out of his all-red Cadillac C6. Tone had on a black and red Jordan sweat suit and all black #3 Jordan's. Tone was from the Southside of Joliet. He had the section of town for the Vice Lords. Tone was twenty-eight, six feet two, 250 pounds, dark skinned, and wore a low cut with waves and a goatee.

Tone could hear music as he walked up to the door of the salon. He opened the door and one of Cardi B's latest hits sounded throughout the system. The women sat and talked and laughed among themselves. Some waited for their turn and others were already in the chair getting their hair styled. Tone walked past two women who were talking about someone else's choice of hair do. He just shook his head and smiled. He thought to himself, "women will always criticize one another's choice of hair style and clothing." Then he noticed a few of the women checking him out. Even though they knew whose man he was. The salon was packed, and all ten chairs were being occupied. Even JaRonda's, but she was nowhere in sight. Tone walked back to the office to see if she was there, but she wasn't. Once again fear started to rise within him. He closed the door and look around until he spotted Donnesha.

Donnesha and JaRonda were best friends. They grew up together. When Tone opened the salon for JaRonda, he advised her to bring Donnesha along. She ran the salon whenever JaRonda wasn't around. Donnesha was light skinned and on the heavy side. She was extremely cute and filled with self-confidence. One day her hair may be blonde and cut short and the next day it may be green with long weave.

Tone called out, "Don Don!" She looked up smiled and waved at him. Tone beckoned for her to come over to where he was standing by the office door. Donnesha excused herself from her client and walked over to him.

"Hey! I didn't know you all were back." She said as she hugged Tone.

Tone looked at her strangely and said, "What do you mean, you didn't know we were back? You haven't seen JaRonda this morning?" He was now being overwhelmed with fear and anxiety. "Her car is parked outside in her spot."

"What? I've been here all morning. She hasn't come in. I opened up and haven't been anywhere since then." Donnesha said with a concerned tone. She noticed the anguish in Tone's face.

"Her car is out there, and I know she wouldn't have gone anywhere without at least coming in to tell you where she was going. Plus, she doesn't move without her cell phone. It's glued to her hand." Tone said out loud not really directing it towards Donnesha, but more to himself. He looked down at his watch. Ten fifteen displayed on the watch. He looked at his phone to check what time it was when he started trying to call JaRonda. The last time he tried it had been over an hour ago. Tone pulled Donnesha into the office. "Listen and listen good. I want you to close up as soon as the last woman is done". Donnesha started to worry, and it was now showing on her face.

"Have you seen the news this morning?"

"No, I haven't had time to do much of anything since I opened up. Why? What's wrong? What's going on Tone?" She didn't know what was going on. But she knew it was something serious. It had Tone roused and her best friend missing. Whatever she had missed on the news must have been important. She was frightened and wanted to know what was going on. "Tone, please tell me what's going on? Has something happened to my friend, my sister?" She asked with tears flowing. Donnesha knew the life that Tone lived and wasn't too thrilled when JaRonda told her she was dating him. Plus, everybody in the hood knew that Tone and Jake's crew didn't get along. Donnesha reflected to a time when JaRonda and she were in Applebee's with Tone and one of his guys. Jake, Mike, and another guy walked in and there was tension. Words were thrown back and forth, and guns were pulled.

"Hey, get it together! This is still a place of business. I don't want the customers to get afraid or anything. Listen, Jacinta and her son were shot earlier today."

"What?! No... no... Are you sure? Are they alright?" Donnesha asked as she held her hand over her mouth trying to control her emotions at the same time. She paused, thought to herself, then asked Tone. "Jay Jay doesn't think you had anything to do with that. Does he? Tone, you didn't, right?" She waited but he never responded. Then she yelled, "Tone! Tell me you didn't!" She stared at him with fear in her eyes.

Tone turned and walked away from Donnesha, but she grabbed him by the arm. Tone didn't look back. He just waited to hear what she had to say. "Tone, I have a bad feeling that he does. Y'all have been beef'n for so long and it has never been any peace between you two. Plus, you two have been trying to kill each other." Donnesha breathed in and released it slowly. Then asked. "What do you need me to do? Do you need me to call the police and make up a story?" As she spoke Tone thought to himself how he could best deal with this situation. "Tone let me make myself clear. I don't approve of how you or Jake live your lives. But if he has my sister, you'd better do everything in your power to get her back. If he hurts her, you'd better hurt him back. Look at me! I mean it!" She said with an angry look. She fixed her face and clothes and walked out of the door. Tone followed behind.

Tone walked out through the salon and texted on his phone. Donnesha received a text. She read it." No, don't call the cops. I got this." Donnesha laid the phone down as she watched Tone walk out of the salon.

Tone sat in his car and texted someone else. The receiver of the text read. "Get the guys together and meet me at the spot. ASAP!"

Tone received a message back that read, "Bet. Do we need to come heavy?"

"Nah, just come and I'll holla at y'all about it then."

He pulled up in front of a house on Water Street. A few minutes later, three black SUVs pulled up. There were four guys that exited each one. The door opened to the house to where Tone was sitting in a chair having a drink. They all walked over to him and greeted him and each other with handshakes (displaying the gang sign they represented).

"What's up Boss? Man, my fault. I missed the package. I got somebody running the Fed-X truck down right now as we speak. We will get the shipment." Big Tee stated to his boss. He had not been at the shop when the Fed-X truck arrived with their shipment from Mexico.

Tone sat and listened to Big Tee go on about how he was going to make sure he made it right. Tone poured himself another drink and then looked big Tee in the eyes and said, "Enough with that. We will not worry about that right now. We have a bigger problem." Big Tee and the other guys thought, what could be a bigger problem than losing a large quantity of drugs, worth hundreds of thousands. Tone then said, "Somebody shot Jake's wife and son. Now Ja-Ronda is missing. I believe Jake has her somewhere. I think. No! I know he thinks I am behind it. I would if it were me. If anybody in this room knows anything, you need to speak up now. Because if I find out later that somebody in this family did it, and didn't let me know, Jake is going to be the least of your problems. Because now my wife and unborn child are missing. Do I make myself clear?" Tone asked as he threw the glass he had into the wall. Tone stood up and yelled, "Do I make myself clear?! Because I haven't heard any of you say I have!" Tone looked around the room at his guys. His eyes red and chest heaved up and down.

The men said in unison, "Yes, Lord. You have made yourself clear."

"So, what are we going to do? Are we going up to the hospital, to holler at dude?" Asked Big Tee. Tone sat back and thought to himself.

"Have Michelle go by and pick my mom up. Then tell her to take mom to Ke'Andra's school and take her out of class. Take them to the safe house." Michelle is one of the chicks that runs with the crew. She is known for dating ballers and setting them up to be robbed by Tone's crew once she finds out their business. Also, she knows how to handle a weapon. "Let her know what's up. Tell her to stay with them until I say different. And send a few more guys too." Tone gave the order. "That sounds like a good idea. Tee, just you and I are going to go to the hospital. The rest of you get out there and find out what you can. Whatever you find out, hit me, and let me know. Don't make a move. Understood?!"

"Boss, dude 'dun' lost his mind. If he thinks you had anything to do with it, he might flip out. You really think it's a good idea that we don't go packing?" Big Tee is Tone's right-hand man and chief enforcer. He play's no games when it comes down to it. When it was time to move, he was always on the front line and ready for battle. He knew that Tone loved his wife and child more than anything. Plus, Tone always had his back and made sure his family was good while he did time in the federal pin.

"Nah, my wife and unborn child's lives, are on the line. I need to show him I had nothing to do with this. Plus, we need to put all this old mess behind us. Starting today. It's been too much killing between us for far too long. Now somebody is really trying to get us to kill one another by making a move on his family. And I know in my heart that he has JaRonda somewhere, if he hasn't already killed her." Tone wanted his crew to get a clear understanding that things were about to change. They all walked out of the house and loaded back into the SUV's. Tone jumped in with Big Tee and everybody went on to their destination.

## GONE TOO SOON
## AHMAUD ARBERY
### YOUNG BLACK MAN WAS JOGGING AND HIS LIFE WAS TAKEN BY A RETIRED COP AND HIS SON.

# CHAPTER EIGHT

Donnesha went back to doing her client's head, but her mind was far from her work.

"Don Don. Are you alright?" Asked her client, Alicia.

"Uh? Um, yeah, I am fine. I was just paying attention to the news." She lied and said, "It is crazy what is going on out there in the streets. People are protesting all over the world behind these cops killing unarmed blacks." Donnesha was trying to keep her mind focused on her work and off JaRonda, but that was hard to do. She kind of wished that Tone hadn't said anything to her but would have been mad if he hadn't. Donnesha was all messed up in the head.

"Girl, yes. My husband," Donnesha rolled her eyes and twisted up her lips at the statement of, 'My husband'. She knew the truth about their relationship. Troy, the man Alicia referred to as her husband was the father to her two kids. Troy was also known in the streets for having relationships with multiple women. Alicia knew also, but he is spoiling her, and she has always been known for being naïve when it came to him. She acts as though they are the per-

..e. But Donnesha and others, know better. .f Donnesha's other clients is also one of Troy's .oy mommas. However, it is none of Donnesha's business. She just keeps her mouth shut when the women speak of Troy like he is the perfect man.

Alicia proceeded to speak. "Troy had to have the talk with our sons about what to do if they got pulled over by the police. It is a shame that we as a people must have that talk. White parents don't have to worry about if their child gets pulled over whether it will be their last time breathing. When we get pulled over for a simple traffic stop, we don't know if that will be our last day on this earth. It's just crazy. When I see a police officer behind me, I get scared like I have something to hide."

As Alicia went on and on, Donnesha's mind went back to thinking about the safety of her best friend/sister. She couldn't even concentrate. Every time the door to the shop opened, she would look over in hopes that it was JaRonda.

"Don. Girl, are you sure you are alright? Because you don't seem like yourself and you haven't said a word. That isn't like you."

"I am sorry. I just have a lot on my mind right now, Donnesha stated.

Alicia turned around in her seat to face Donnesha and said, "Girl, I saw the news this morning. I also noticed that you haven't been the same since you came back from speaking with Tone. Please tell me that Tone didn't have anything to do with the shooting. We all know about the beef between he and Jay. They haven't gotten alone since high school. I've known them for years. They both are sweet and kind men, but they are also dangerous. I would hate to think that Tone's hatred for Jay Jay would cause him to shoot a woman and her child."

Donnesha didn't say a word. She knew that Alicia was trying to get some info out of her to go and spread.

"Nah girl. You know Tone wouldn't do anything like that. He keeps his street business in the streets and between whomever he has beef with. You sound crazy for even thinking it," Donnesha said with a touch of attitude in her voice. "I am just dealing with this dude who must think I am boo boo the fool." She figured she would give her something to go and gossip about that wouldn't cause anyone to get hurt. Plus, Donnesha wasn't even in a relationship at the moment. "Girl you know how these fools can act when they think they got you on lock."

"Girl, who are you telling?" They both laughed but Donnesha's was a fake laugh. Alicia asked, "So, what did he do?" Donnesha shook her head because she knew she was going to be nosey.

"He doesn't think I know he's been creeping around." Then gave Alicia a look like, you know what I mean.

"What?! Girl, I know he ain't? I know you are going to check him. Girl, it couldn't be me. I don't play that." Donnesha stood behind her and said to herself, "Whatever."

"Who is this dog? You have kept him a secret. I tell you everything and you haven't told me anything about this dude."

Before Donnesha could respond and tell another lie, the news came with an update. One of the women that work in the shop cut the music down and turned the TV up. The reporter talked about the shooting and showed a picture of Jacinta. She explained that she suffered minor injuries, but her child had a 30 percent chance of making it. She went on to report about little Jake's injuries.

Some of the women's mouths dropped when they heard the news and couldn't believe what they heard. Some even wiped tears from their faces. They were whispering with each other. Some pulled out their cell phone and went online to read the comments. Donnesha noticed that some of the women were peeking over at her as they talked amongst themselves.

Donnesha knew exactly what they were thinking, and that was Tone was behind the shooting.

Some of the women got up and walked out of the shop without saying a word. She felt where they were coming from. Nobody wanted to be in the middle of any beef between Jake and Tone. She knew that they were afraid that at any moment, someone might come and shoot up the shop. Trying not to reveal her emotions, she felt the same way. Donnesha couldn't wait until the last client was done, so she could close the shop.

THE ARE FOUR KIDS WHOSE LIVES
WILL NEVER BE THE SAME BECAUSE
THEIR MOTHER'S, CHARLEENA LYLES,
LIFE WAS TAKEN BY A COP!

# Chapter Nine

Jake stood beside his wife as they watched their child fight for his life. The conversation between Jake and Bishop Walker kept replaying in his mind. He still wasn't convinced that God really does exist. Nevertheless, when Bishop said that he and Jacinta, we're making the wrong decision, it puzzled him. He still wrestled within himself about what he was going to do when he finds out who was behind the shooting. Jake's thoughts were interrupted when Shanon appeared in the doorway.

"Hey Fam, I am about to make a run. I have some business I need to handle." Shanon said, as he stuck his head into the ICU to inform Jake. Jake turned to face his cousin and could see that Shanon didn't seem like himself. Before he could respond, Shanon had rushed back out of the room. Jake though that it was weird that Shanon didn't acknowledge Jacinta, knowing this was the first time he'd seen her.

Jake turned and said, "Ah, something's not right. Shanon seems like he is hiding something. I'll be back. Let me go and catch him and find out what's really going on. Then Jake rushed out of the room behind Shanon. As he turned the corner, he could hear Shanon on the phone and the conversation sounded heated. Shanon reached the elevator and pushed the button. When the doors opened, he stepped in and texted Mike. Jake called out for Shanon to hold the door. Shanon looked when he heard Jake's voice, but he let the door close as he watched Jake come towards him. Jake thought that strange, as he stood in the middle of the hall. Shanon had more than enough time to keep the doors from closing. Jake wondered if he had found out something about the shooting and was just keeping it from him? Or did Shanon know more than he had said? Jake pulled out his phone and tried to call Shanon. He just got his voicemail. He texted Shanon and waited, but never received a text back. Jake returned to his wife and didn't say a word. Jacinta could tell that something was on his mind. She was too focused on little Jake to concern herself with Jake right then.

Shanon approached his car and looked to see if Jake was following behind him. Once in the car, he made a call and sped out of the hospital's lot. He made his way to the interstate.

Shanon's cell began to ring. He noticed that it was another call from Jake. A few text messages from him came through saying, call ASAP. He laid the phone back down. As he reached his exit, Shanon made a call. He spoke to the recipient in an angry tone. "How did you mess this up?! I worked too hard to set this up and too long for you to come along and ruin it!" Shanon shook his head. "What do you mean you can still take care of it?! It's too late. I needed that handled today, not later! Where is my money? I will be there shortly, and you better have every single dime, or I'ma put two in your head!" Shanon ended the call and threw his phone down beside him. His blood was boiling as he gripped the steering wheel.

As he pulled on to the ramp, he noticed the same unmarked car from earlier. Shanon pulled into a BP station. He jumped out and pretended to pump gas. He watched to see what they were going to do. They rode past but not without looking over at him. Once out of sight, Shanon jumped back into his car and sped off in another direction. Twenty minutes later, Shanon pulled up to a large house and jumped out of his car. He tucked his weapon into his waist. Shanon banged on the door. Seconds later, a young white female opened the door and pointed as she stepped aside. She could see nothing but anger in his eyes. He came back out with two duffel bags and placed them in the trunk of his car. He sent a text before he pulled out of the driveway.

Mike was sitting in the living room with JaRonda when he received the text from Shanon. Mike walked into the kitchen. He read the text and then called Shanon. "Yeah, what's up fam?" Shanon asked?

"Not much just babysitting."

"Man, you haven't killed her yet?" Shanon asked playfully.

"Man, I want to." Mike said as he looked at Ja-Ronda who was able to hear the conversation. Mike had his phone on speaker.

"Bruh, I got the money back. I wanted to put one in his hand. I don't know how they messed that up. Everything was planned to the 'T'."

"Man, I don't understand either." Mike said.

"Hey, word on the street is that she's missing. Tone's guys are out asking around. Plus, he got $25,000 for any info for her whereabouts. Dude doesn't have a clue what's going on. I found out from ole girl. The chick he'd been messing with. You know the one I put on him." Shanon said as he laughed. Mike looked up to see the expression on JaRonda's face when she heard this new info about her husband and another woman.

"Hey Bruh. You should see this chick's face. It's priceless. I have the phone on speaker, and she just heard you saying Tone is smashing ole girl. She looks pitiful." Mike said as he laughed.

"Oh well. She'll be alright."

"Hey just put the money back up. How is Jake holding up?" Mike asked.

"Man, I don't know. I haven't been back there with him. He keeps calling and texting me ever since I bounced. We need to figure out something because when cuz finds out the truth, he is going to lose it." Shanon said with concern in his voice...

"We'll figure it out and he will never know. I'ma make a few calls and see what I can come up with. Go back to the hospital. We need to know soon as things change."

"Alright, I am on my way back up there. I will let you know something as soon as I do." Shanon said as he jumped back onto the interstate.

PHILANDO CASTILE

A BLACK FATHER GONE TOO SOON.
KILLED BY A COP.

# CHAPTER TEN

Eleven a.m. Jake had been at the hospital with his family and friends for a couple of hours and there still wasn't any change in little Jake's condition. Even though Jake had some hope and inspiration after receiving the word of God from Bishop Walker, he still had crazy thoughts running through his head. He knew what Bishop had said, but he just couldn't let it go. What really had him thinking was Shanon. He just could not get over the feeling that Shanon knew something. Jake has always been right when he felt this way. He hated the thought that his very own blood could be behind the shooting or know something and not tell him.

Jacinta could tell that something was really bothering him and grabbed his hand and asked. "Jake, what is it? You've been tense and I know when something is bothering you. And don't tell me it's about little Jake because there is something else on your mind." She stared at him and waited for him to respond.

But to her surprise Jake said, "it's something going on, and Shanon isn't telling me what he knows." He turned and stared back at her and said, "I'm having one of those feelings. You know when I do, I am rarely wrong. I think Shanon is behind this." Jacinta's eyes widen and she grabbed her chest.

"No, Jake! He wouldn't try and kill us, certainly not, you. Your feeling is wrong. This is one of those rare times." Jacinta said as she shook her head back and forth.

"Listen to me. When I went after him, I could hear him on his phone fussing at someone. When I told him to hold the elevator door, he looked at me and let them close without trying to stop it. I've been calling him and texting. He's not getting back to me. When have you ever known him not to get right back?" Jake asked. Jacinta just sat there in disbelief. "I hit Mike and asked him if he had heard from him. He said no. Something is up! Trust and believe, I am going to get to the bottom of it. I just pray that I am wrong because I will hate to have to kill my own cousin."

"Oh no you're not! If you are right, and we find out it's him, we will let the law deal with him." Before Jacinta finished Jake jumped up.

"The law?! Not going to do that. I'ma handle that myself. Try and kill me or mine! You have to go. I don't care who it is!" Jake said as he hit his fist against his chest.

"Jake! Shut the hell up! If you kill him or whoever, you're killing my baby. Our baby. Your son. Little Jake. So, shut up and stop talking crazy! I said we're going to let the law handle it. No matter who it is. OK? I hope it's not Shanon, but if it is, he will pay for it. Let God handle it." Jacinta said as she pulled Jake back down into his seat and wrapped her arms around him. She knew how much he loved Shanon and she prayed that it wouldn't be him or anybody else. She hoped that they would get that person or persons before Jake and them found out. Even though Jake knew what was said she knew that doubt remained in his heart about God. And he would make it painful for whoever shot them.

Jake laid with his head on Jacinta's shoulder and thought about the words spoken to him. He knew that Jacinta would suffer for years like his mother and auntie. Then he thought about how his family would feel if he killed his cousin. But how would they feel if they found out he was behind it? Jake's emotions were all mixed up. The thought that Shanon could be responsible for their pain filled him with anger and sadness.

While Jake and Jacinta sat in the ICU, two detectives walked into the waiting area. The leading detective was a 29-year-old young lady, dressed in a two-piece navy-blue pantsuit with a white button-down shirt and black loafers. There was a Chrome 45 service piece on her hip. Her partner was a very tall black male who also had a Chrome service piece. He was dressed in a gray suit, white shirt, gray tie, and black loafers.

Shanon stood up when they walked into the waiting area. He created a barrier between them, the family, and where Jake and Jacinta were. Shanon knew exactly who they were and why they were there. "Can I help you?" Shannon asked as he mean mugged them.

"No. You can't help me. I am not here to talk to you." Detective LaKesha Foulks seriously warned. "I am here to talk to Mr. and Mrs. Johnson and you're not either of them. Now would you please step aside before I arrest you for obstruction of justice." She looked at him and said, "Your move. What are you going to do?"

Before Shannon could respond, two handsome young men approached them dressed in Armani suits and carrying leather briefcases. The duo stepped in between Shanon and the officers. The oldest of the two handed the detective a card that read,'Waithe and family attorney at law'. Then he said to her. "Hello. My name is Marcus Waithe. This is my brother and partner Derek Waithe, Jr. We are here on behalf of the Johnson family. If you don't mind telling us the issue, we would be obliged to help or set an appointment for you to speak with Mrs. Johnson, not Mr. Johnson. There is no need, seeing that he wasn't there. He would not be able to help you in anyway." The family looked around at one another trying to figure out why the detectives were asking to speak with Jake?

While the lawyers talked with the detectives, Shanon went to the ICU to inform Jake what was happening. Seconds later Jake burst into the waiting area. Shanon followed behind pushing Jacinta in a wheelchair. He said, "What?! What the hell do y'all want?! Uh?!" Jake was boiling.

His mother stepped in front of him to keep him from getting too close to the officer. It's no secret that detective Foulks had been trying to get something on Jake for years. "Calm down baby. Not here. This isn't the time or the place. Being angry isn't going to help the situation. They are here just doing their job. If you don't wish to talk to them, let the lawyers handle it. They have it under control." She said as she held Jake's hand. Jake had so much disdain for the police especially Detective Foulks. He hadn't heard a word his mother said.

Jake pulled away from her and walked towards Detective Foulks and said, "Follow me." He walked her back to the ICU and pointed at the window towards his son who was laid out on a bed with machines regulating his vitals. "Now tell me what you want? Why are you here when you should be out trying to find the ones responsible for my son lying in there with three bullet wounds in his five-year-old chest? Instead, you are here harassing me trying to find out things that you will never get out of me. If I, knew any…" Jake was interrupted by his attorney.

"That's enough Jake. Don't say another word." His attorney Marcus instructed.

The detective turned around and said, "Mrs. Johnson, I am so deeply sorry about your baby. I can only imagine what you must be going through right now. I promise you that I will do my best to find out who's behind this." She then walked out of the ICU. Once back in the waiting area, she told her partner, "We're finished here. Let's go. We have work to do." They headed out toward the elevator.

Back in the ICU Jake noticed that Shanon was texting and wondered who and why he was texting. As he walked towards him, Marcus and Derek pulled Jake to the side and asked if they could have a word with him. "Mr. Johnson, our father sends his prayers and blessings. Immediately after he heard about the attack on your family, he called us and insisted we come right over. He said to tell you that he's sorry that he could not be here because he and his wife were on their way to Paris. We were told to bring the guys with us for security. They're here to handle anything you need done. They've been instructed to let no one through those doors without your permission. He also said to pull this out of the safe and bring it to you." Derek handed Jake an envelope. "He said you would know what it's all about and that the pilot is on standby to fly you anywhere in or out of the country."

Mr. Waithe had done federal time and knew Jake's father. Back before going to prison, he used to supply Jake's father with drugs and weapons. Upon his release, he sent his sons to law school and opened a law firm geared towards representing men and women who had pending criminal charges to secure they had a fighting chance. The envelope had account numbers to Jake's overseas accounts, passports, and new identities for him, Jacinta, and little Jake.

"We will stay around for a while; in case you need anything. Please let us know and it will be taken care of. Our father said that if need be, he would cut his trip short to accommodate you and your family."

"Thanks a lot, but right now I'm good for the most part. It's good to have you all here though." They shook hands and the attorneys walked back to the waiting area.

Once the attorneys were out of sight, Jake called out to Shanon. Shanon turned around and walked towards Jake and stuck his cell back into his pocket. "What's up, cuz?" Shanon said.

"What's up? You tell me." He said as he walked up on Shanon. Shanon could hear the aggressive tone in Jake's voice.

"What you mean?" Shanon looked confused.

"Where you been? And why didn't you call me like I said.?" By this time Jake was in Shanon's face.

"Fam, I don't know what's on your mind, but you need to step back." He pushed Jake

and said, "I know you have a lot on your mind, but I don't know why you are stepping to me like this. So, I am going to let it slide. But you're tripping." By this time, they had gotten kind of loud.

"You going to let what slide? Let me…" Before Jake could finish, he was interrupted by his mother and aunt.

"What is going on? We can hear you two all the way in the waiting room. Now what is it?" Denise asked as she looked back and forth at her son and nephew.

"It's nothing momma." Shanon said before walking away.

"It's something, because you two are acting like fools," Jake's mother said as she looked at her son.

"It's nothing like he said." Jake turned around and walked back into the ICU.

Ruby and Denise stood there and watched as their sons walked away. There was no doubt in their minds that something was terribly wrong.

Denise turned to Ruby and said, "They just lied to our faces." Ruby nodded in agreement. "I don't know what's going on Sis, but the devil is a lie. He is trying to tear our boys apart. I can feel it in my spirit. So, we're going to go to the Chapel, put on our spiritual armor, touch, and agree according to the word of God, and bind this devil." Ruby said, "Lets, go."

TAMIR RICE AGE 12

ALYANA STANLEY-JONES AGE 7

DARNESHA HARRIS AGE 17

WE WILL NEVER KNOW WHO THESE BABIES COULD HAVE BEEN IN LIFE OR WHAT THEY COULD HAVE DONE TO CHANGE THIS WORLD, BECAUSE THEIR LIVES WERE TAKEN BY THOSE WHO WERE TO PROTECT THEM. COPS!

# CHAPTER ELEVEN

Det. Foulks waited for the elevator doors to open. Her partner noticed that she was overly tense. When the doors opened, they stepped inside, and Det. Foulks broke down.

Her partner Det. Wallace asked. "What's wrong?" As he tried to pull her up to her feet. She had slipped down and was bent over crying.

"Once this case is solved, I am done. I'm quitting the force. I can't do this anymore. I went in there trying to trip Jake up. I didn't care about their family's feelings. That family is hurting and hurting badly. Their five-year-old child has three bullet wounds in his chest. He is fighting for his life. And all I could hope for was that Jake incriminate himself so, I could finally lock him up. I wasn't caring about his feelings or his wife's. This isn't for me. I know better than to have hate in my heart for a person no matter who he is or what he has done. I can't call myself a Christian. It's not right to hate and be uncaring. I had no compassion. But when I saw that baby hooked up to that life support machine, it was over. I wanted to break down then." Det. Foulks cried even harder. She's a mother of two twin girls the same age as Jake Jr. She couldn't erase the picture of little Jake out of her mind. She thought how that could have been one of her children lying there.

Her partner didn't say a word. He handed her his handkerchief. She used it to wipe away the evidence of her emotional episode from her face. Before the doors opened, she stood up and looked deep into her partners eyes and said, "You better not tell a soul what you saw today or there will be another unsolved shooting." The doors opened to the lobby. She stepped out. Detective Wallace stood there for a moment before proceeding to follow behind. "Come on. What are you waiting for? We have a lot of work to do. I promise that I will find out who is behind this. I always keep my word." She said after seeing him still standing there.

The two detectives sat in the car. Det. Foulks was in a very deep meditation. Her partner didn't say a word. He thought she was still dealing with what she had just seen. Det. Foulks turned and said to her partner, "there is something we missed. We overlooked something. We need to go back to the scene."

Det. Wallace said, "I feel like that's going to be a waste of time. We had a dozen men and women out there for hours. If they didn't find anything there's nothing to find."

Det. Foulks shot him a look that sent chills through him. If looks could kill he would be dead. Then she spat. "That's what's wrong with this younger generation. You want the promotions, benefits, and everything else that comes along with being a detective but don't want to do any leg work." She rolled her eyes and turned the key over, put the car in gear, and sped off. The ride back to Richmond Ave and Black Road was incredibly quiet. Det. Wallace felt like he had said enough and was tired of her insults. He said to himself that he would just let nature take its course.

Fifteen minutes later they pulled up to the scene and everything had been cleaned up. They parked the car and got out. The area was back to normal just that fast. Det. Wallace smiled. He just knew that they weren't going to find anything. Det. Foulks said as she pointed, "you walk that way and look for anything out of place." The detective shook his head and walked in the direction she pointed to; still thinking that this was a waste of time.

Det. Foulks walked and looked around and didn't say anything. She was determined to prove her point and not permit her partner the satisfaction of providing his. But after a few minutes had passed, she was starting to doubt. Then she looked up and her determination had paid off. She smiled and called Det. Wallace over. Once he came and stood beside her, she pointed up and said, "Is that what I think it is?" As she smiled. There was a traffic cam. The city of Joliet had just installed them a week earlier. "Bingo! That is what we had overlooked. Now that is what you call real old school detective work. You always follow your gut."

Det. Wallace just stared at the traffic Cam. He didn't know what to say. He hated that she was right because he knew she wasn't going to let him live it down. However, he was please to know that they had something to go on to work the case.

"Come on! Why are you always standing around? We have work to do." Det. Foulks said with a smirk on her face as she walked back to the car. "Lunch is on you."

"Alright, you were right." Det. Wallace said as he walked towards the car with his hands in the air. Once in the car, he didn't even make eye contact with her, but he could see that smirk on her face. He pulled out his phone and called the station. He wanted all the footage from the day's events pulled up by the time they reached the station.

# CHAPTER TWELVE

Tone and Big Tee we're headed west on Interstate 80 to go and have a talk with Jake. Tone sat very quietly in his seat. He was thinking about JaRonda and the baby's well- being. His mind was everywhere. He didn't know if she was still alive or what. Knowing that he and Jake were two of kind, he knew it was possible that she could really be dead. He wondered if she suffered, if she was dead, and where was her body. He tried to think positively but he knew how he would have handled things.

By coming to Jake without his crew or weapons, Tone hoped that Jake would realize that he had nothing to do with the assault on his family. He hoped that if he had JaRonda stored up somewhere he would return her to him safely.

Twelve noon they pulled into St. Joseph's parking lot. Tone looked at his phone and saw that he had a text message from Donnesha asking about JaRonda. He didn't respond back. Big Tee looked over at his boss/friend. He noticed that Tone had dried up tear spots. "Hey man don't worry. We are going to get Ja-Ronda back or die trying. I got your back all the way to the grave. If this fool does not realize that you or any of us did not have anything to do with this, we'll handle it. An eye for and eye." Big Tee tried to console his boss and ease his nerves as they sat in the truck.

Tone got himself together, made sure his face was clean, and stepped out of the SUV. Tone and Big Tee walked into the hospital lobby with anger displayed on their faces. The same little old lady saw them coming. She picked up the phone and called security. She warned them to keep an eye on their monitors. She hung the phone up as they came closer to her.

"Hello gentlemen. How may I help you today?"

"We need to know where's the intensive care unit." Tone said as he stood in front of the lady with dark shades on.

She stared back at him and asked. "Are you here for someone in particular? Maybe I can help you."

Tone looked at the lady for a second before he spoke. "Yeah. We're here for the Johnson family. Now will you please direct us to the right location, or should we find it ourselves?" After speaking, he leaned over the counter and took his shades off. He looked her straight in the eyes like he was trying to read her soul. She looked around Tone and towards Big Tee. She pointed to the elevator.

"Take it to the third floor, get off, and go to your right. You can't miss it."

"Thank you, ma'am. You have been a big help. Keep up the good work." Big Tee said as they walked away.

Tone began feeling weak after he stepped onto the elevator. Thoughts of JaRonda were plaguing his mind. Soon he would be face to face with the man who believed he had something to do with the attack on his wife and child. Tone wasn't the least bit afraid of Jake, but not knowing the whereabouts and condition of his wife had him a little less than 100%. Tone knew how he would react if he was in Jake's situation.

Once they stepped off the elevator, they walked down the hallway and right into the waiting area. Soon as Shanon spotted Tone, he jumped to his feet and said, "I know this dude didn't." Then he ran up on Tone and said, "You have a lot of nerve showing up here!" As he got closer, everyone else knew that it was going to be a problem and were shocked that Tone had come.

"I come in peace. I just want to talk to…" Before Tone could finish Shanon cut him off.

"What?! What?! What the hell do you have to talk to Jake about. Uh?! You want to tell him how you tried to kill his family?!" Shanon yelled in Tone's face. Big Tee stepped in between them. Big Tee could see the rage in Shanon's eyes. Shanon asked him. "What?! What?!" as he got even closer to Big Tee. "You trying to do something nigga?" The two men were nose to nose. The security that had been sent to protect Jake's family got in position and were ready to move when needed. Marcus reached around and pulled out a small three-eighty caliber pistol. He held it in his hand behind his briefcase. His brother walked to the ICU to inform Jake what was going on.

"It is what it is Shanon." Big Tee said.

"Tee we're not here for that. You know that." By the time he got his words out Shanon caught Big Tee with a right to the jaw. Big Tee stumbled back and shook it off and returned a blow to Shanon directly in the mouth. Shanon threw another right and catches Tee in the left eye. The two men rushed each other. Tee grabbed Shanon and slammed him to the floor. The two went back and forth with throwing each other all over the waiting area and landing blow for blow.

There was screaming from Shanon's mother and aunt to stop. The men in the waiting room tried to break them up. The two large men were not stopping. Somebody was going to have to give up or it was going to take an act of God to break them apart. There have been years of hatred between the two crews and today it had reached its boiling point. Even though Tone had command that Big Tee stop, it was to no avail.

Moments later Jake came rushing into the room with Derek and Jacinta in toe. The waiting area was a mess. Chairs and tables were everywhere. The room was full of hospital security. Shanon and Big Tee had been separated. They still shouted back and forth at one another. Jacinta's mother pulled her to the side. Bishop Walker and Joe ran and held Jake back trying to deescalate the situation. Jake still tried to get to Tone all the while cussing him and saying what he was going to do. Jake could not hear a thing. All he was focused on was the man he had hated for years. Now they were face to face. Jake had forgotten about the words that had been spoked to him by the man of God.

All he thought about was that the one responsible was now standing in his face and was there to taunt him.

"It's over for you Tone. I'ma kill you! You went after my family! You know you are a dead man and can't nobody stop me!" Jake yelled out as he still tried to get to Tone. Jake's mother stepped over to him and tried to get him to calm down. But she saw a look in her son's eyes that she had only seen before in his father's. She knew that there was no talking him down. "I am going to kill your whole family. There will not be one of you left." Jake worked himself free from the bishop and his father-in-law. Once Jake was free, he pulled his gun and pointed it at Tone. Shanon pulled his and pointed it at Big Tee. The hospital security pulled their weapons and Jake's security pulled theirs and pointed it at the hospital's security. The waiting area got extremely quiet. Members from the church ducked for cover.

No one said a word. Seconds seemed like minutes. Everyone was in shock. Jake and Shanon's mothers tried their best to persuade them to put the guns away. But the hatred in their hearts had taken over. Shanon never took his eyes off Big Tee and Jake was fixed on Tone. Then from the back of the room the silence was broken when Jacinta yelled. "Stop! Stop! Stop... it! Enough! Jake put that gun away! You too Shanon. I can't take it anymore. I have had enough! Jake, you know if you kill him, you're killing Little Jake. I am tired of this. Tone I don't know why you are even here. If there is something you want to say, please say it and go. I need to get back to my baby." Jacinta was crying. Her mother and father wrapped their arms around her. "This has gotten out of hand. My son is back there breathing by a machine, and you all are up here acting a fool. All this hatred must stop, and it must stop today! I mean today! Tone is here for a reason, for whatever that is. But you are going to listen. Do you understand? Jake! Do you understand?!" Jake looked at his wife. He could see the pain in her eyes. He dropped his hand and held the gun to his side. Shanon did the same. The men that were sent to protect Jake and his family put away their weapons. The hospital security held theirs to their side. "Go ahead Tone, tell him what it is you want to say."

Tone opened his jacket and spun around to show that he was unarmed. Big Tee did the same. "Thank you, Jacinta. Jake, man I'm so sorry for what happened to your family today. I got my guys out there trying to find out information. When I saw the news, I knew you were going to think that I had something to do with it. For real, bruh. It wasn't me. I need you to believe me. That's why I am here unarmed and without my guys." Tone dropped his head, took a breath, and said, "Man, my wife is missing." Everyone's breath was taken away. A sinking feeling came over Jacinta. She thought to herself that she hadn't seen Mike all day. Then she thought about what she had told Jake and he said he was already on top of it. That meant Mike is the one with JaRhonda or knows something about it. "As soon as I saw the news, I called her cell and the salon. I didn't get an answer on either. So, I went to the salon and saw her car parked but she wasn't anywhere insight." The more Tone spoke the more upset he became. Jake's mother and aunt looked at their sons in disbelief. They knew who their kids were but never thought that they would have been capable of something like this. Jacinta knew she had told Jake to call off whatever he had going on once Jake shared Bishop Walker's conversation with her. He never once mentioned to her that he had already captured someone. Now, knowing that whatever actions he made could cause the death of their child, made her sick to her stomach. The thought that Jake had JaRonda somewhere afraid for her life and that of her unborn child, made Jacinta feel compassion for Tone. "We just flew back in the country last night. We renewed our vows." Tone broke down and began to cry. "I know we have had bad blood between the two of us. I made a vow to my wife that I would try and make peace with you. I am out of the game, and I am turning the enterprise over to my man Tee. I don't want him to inherit my stress and problems. I just cannot see myself living this life any more or dying in those streets. When I get into my car, I don't know if it is going to blow up or if I will make it back home. I just want to get old and watch my children grow into the people they will become. I want to be able to give my daughter away on her wedding day. I want to be a grandfather." Tone said as he stared into Jake's eyes.

Jacinta got up from her wheelchair and walked over to Jake, looking him straight in the eyes. He stared back into her red and swollen eyes. She took a deep breath, exhaled, and calmly said. "Jake, honey. Give this man his wife back. You know you are killing our son. You know that he will not pull through this if you don't. Baby, you must let JaRonda go. You said that everything was going to be alright. That God said so! But it cannot as long as you are holding her. You are doing wrong and that wrong will destroy our baby. She's a mother just like me. How would you feel if you did not know what was going on with me, or where I was?" She turned to Tone and grabbed his hand. Jake bit down on his bottom lip just seeing her hold his hand. It fueled his anger. Jacinta said, "I am sorry." She turned back to Jake and said, "Give this man his wife back!" She ordered him for the first time in her life. "I mean it! If my baby dies, this marriage is over. It dies with him. So, loose her Jake, right now." Jacinta stared at him. Jake thought about what Bishop Walker had said about their marriage. Jacinta walked out of the waiting area. Her mother followed behind.

Jake looked around the room at everybody that was waiting to see what he was going to do or say. He looked at Tone with more hatred in his heart. "I don't have your wife. If you know what's best, you and that big punk will leave while you can."

"You heard him." Shanon said. "Or we can get it popp'n in here." By this time Shanon's mother stood up and told all the men to have a seat. She ordered that Shanon and Jake put their weapons away.

"Shanon and Jake, I need to tell you both something that I hoped I never had to. You two are out of control. But that's not your fault. When I was six and Jake your father was eight, your grandfather was a runner for some immensely powerful people down in Mississippi. He drove from county to county moving shipment for them. On one of his runs, he was pulled over by some officers that worked for the competitors. They offered daddy a job. They wanted him to drive for them. Daddy believed in loyalty, and he was loyal to the men he worked for. They paid him well and made sure if he needed anything it was done. He told them about the offer that had been made. They said that they would handle it and not to worry.

Daddy was making a run one night, and the same officers pulled him over. They did not arrest him. They took the shipment and let him go. See by doing that, that made it look like your grandfather was lying and kept the shipment for himself. They knew that he had told them about the offer. What better way to try and get over when you have let it be known that some police tried to get you to work for them. Everybody knew that the cops were crooked, so who better to blame. He told them what had happened. They said that they believed it and would handle it. However, they did not. A few days later after daddy left the house, some men came in and kidnapped momma, your grandmother.

She was missing for three days. When she was found, she was hanging from a tree. Momma had been beaten and raped repeatedly." By that time, Denise and Jake's mother faces were covered with tears. Bishop Walker and Joe both had sorrowful expressions. They knew the story and how it had affected the life of their friend. Mrs. Johnson recalled nights that her husband would wake up in a cold sweat from dreaming about the episode. Denise cried even harder as she thought of her mother. Mother Walker gave both women some tissue. "Jake, your father is the one who found her hanging from the tree. Momma was naked, and daddy knew exactly who was responsible and vowed that the real criminals would pay. The cops knew also. But when you are white and powerful like they were in Mississippi, you could get away with whatever you wanted.

The police locked up a guy. They charged him with the murder. But everyone knew that he was not the one who had done it. He was the town drunk and did not bother anyone. They claimed that the man was covered in blood and had momma's purse on him. He confessed to the crime, but only after they had beat him black and blue. Daddy knew that he was not the one. He was just afraid for his life. Daddy made sure that he would make them pay.

When daddy went to take care of momma's funeral arrangement, the pastor pulled him aside and said for him to let it go. Don't try to get revenge on the real murders. He said that God had full control. If he did not listen, whatever he had planned would bring a generational curse on his family. Jake, your father was a very stubborn man, but had nothing on your grandfather. Dad was hurt deep to the core of his soul to know that your father saw his mother hanging from a tree.

Daddy went after those men one by one. He would wait until they were along somewhere and take them out to the woods and beat them mercilessly. They could only be identified by dental records. Then he would take them to their home and throw them in the yard. He killed four men. During that time, you did not kill four white men and think you were going to get away with it. You were guilty no matter what. That's why we moved up here.

Jake, I am telling you and Shanon this for a reason. It's time for you to step up and break the curse. Jake, your father knew all about this curse. He died just like his father. Neither of them made their peace with God. The curse will continue from generation to generation until one of the men in this family step up and break it.

Jake, baby, you can break it today. You must do what is right. You are a powerful man in the streets, but the real power is when you defeat the devil and his plans. Satan can only win if you let him. You know you hate to loss at anything. So, destroy his works by doing the right thing today. If you have this man's wife, you need to give her back."

Denise took her nephew into her arms and hugged him. She then turned to her son and wiped away his tears. They embraced tightly. Jake stood there. He was filled with mixed emotions. He did not know exactly what to do. But in his heart, he really wanted to let JaRonda go. Jacinta had made it plain about their marriage if anything happened with little Jake. Sadly, his dislike for Tone still controlled him. Shanon looked at him like,

"What's it going to be?" Jake stared at Tone for a minute before turning to walk back to the ICU.

Tone dropped his head and stood to his feet. He said to Big Tee. "Let's go." Bishop Walker went to Tone and grabbed his hand. Tone looked at him with fire in his eyes and said, "I tried to do it the right way. Since he will not turn her over to me, someone is going to die every day." He looked Shanon in the eyes.

Bishop Walker said. "If you just wait and be patient. Maybe he is going back there to tell his wife that he is going to release her. If he really has her. Please have a seat." Tone told Big Tee to have a seat. They will wait to see what Jake is going to do.

# CHAPTER THIRTEEN

Jake stopped and stood against the wall. He knew that he was wrong for continuing to hold JaRonda against her will. Sadly, his pride had a strong hold on him. He loved his family more than anything. He had a 'rep' to maintain. Somebody had to pay. Deep down inside he knew that Tone was telling the truth. Nonetheless, his hatred for Tone had him blind. He could not just let her go and later discover that it was one of Tone's guys trying to prove himself. Listening to the story that his aunt shared, had him really thinking. Her story coincided with what Bishop had previously told him. His father had died. He was Jake's hero. In Jake's eyes his dad could do no wrong. In little Jake's eyes, his dad was his hero. He thought about the hurt and anguish he feels ever so often not having his dad around. He not around to just call and talk with, attend games with, or hang out with on Father's Day. It's even harder on their birthday. Jake's father would always tell him that he was the best birthday gift he'd ever received. Jake was born a week early causing them to have the same birthday. His father was proud to be able to share his day with his son. Jake thought back to when little Jake was born. He wished he could have shared that moment with his dad. He was not able to because his dad was dead. Neither was he there to cheer him on when he played sports.

The day of his and Jacinta's wedding, it was his mother that talked with him to make sure that he was ready to become a husband. She was the only one he could turn to. She did her best to show him how to be a man; from teaching him how to drive to how to shave. Now he was at a cross-road. He did not want his son to feel the way he had felt for many years from the loss of his father.

Jake peered into the ICU and Jacinta stared back at him. She noticed that he had been standing there for a while. She said to him through the glass, "Do the right thing, Jake." She knew that he was struggling with making the right decision. Jake just dropped his head and thought about his son, whom he claimed to be the most important person in his life. His pride seemed to override it all. He looked up to see Shanon coming towards him. Now his thoughts shifted to Shanon and how strange he had been acting.

Shanon walked up and asked. "Cuz, what's up? What are we going to do?" He waited for Jake to respond. He could tell that something was on Jake's mind and asked. "What was that all about earlier?"

Jake raised his head and said."You tell me. You're the one acting strange. I told you to hold up and you looked at me let the door close. I called and texted you and you didn't get back. So, you tell me what's up?" Anger surfaced on Jake's face.

Shanon breathed in and out, shook his head, and said, "Cuz, I was waiting on Tim to call so I could go and pick up the shipment of guns. He said they didn't make it to the 'drop' in time. When he got there, the suppler had left. I was trying to get everything back in order before you found out. You have enough to deal with right now with little man. I went to get the money back. I was not going to tell you. I was just going to set up another appointment and handle it myself. I wanted to kill Tim. I will if this money is short when I count it. I told you we should never have started dealing with that dude anyway." Then Shanon paused and asked. "What did you think was up?" Now anger surfaced on his face as he stared at Jake. "Cuz, don't tell me you thought I knew something about little man and Jacinta getting shot." He waited and Jake did not say a word. "How in the hell could you think something like that?!" Shanon asked as he stepped closer to Jake.

"Did I say that? You said it, not me. But since you brought it up. Do you?!" Jake asked with a serious look in his eyes.

Shanon's chest raised up and down fast as he breathed harder and harder. There was fire in the eyes of both men as they stared one another down.

"Cuz, I can't believe you just asked me something like that. But you have always been like this!"

"Like what?!" Jake asked as he looked up at Shanon.

"Like everything is about you! We're family and you have the nerve to think that I would try and kill Jacinta and Lil man! Nigga, if I wanted you dead, you would be dead." Shanon said, jaws tight and eyes red. He balled his fist but noticed Jacinta watching them. Shanon pointed his finger in Jake's face and said, "You're lucky that we're in this hospital." He looked back at Jacinta. Then turned and walked away. As he walked through the waiting area, he pulled out his phone and texted Mike. "Cuz knows."

# CHAPTER FOURTEEN

Meanwhile, back at the Joliet Police Department, Det. Foulks and Wallace entered with Subway in hand. Det. Foulks spoke out loud. "I had to school this rookie today and show him some old school detective work. He had to buy lunch for doubting me." She laughed and high-fived another old school detective. Det. Wallace just shook his head as they sat down at their desks to eat their lunch.

Det. Foulks sat back and prayed to herself that they would get a lead since she had been boasting. She took a bit of her sandwich, winked at her partner, and said, "Mmmm! Delicious," and smiled.

Det. Wallace shook his head and picked up the phone and called his wife. After remembering how his partner had broken down in the elevator, he just wanted to hear his wife's voice. "Hey bae." He said when she answered. "I was thinking of you and thought that I would call and let you know how much I love and appreciate you." He smiled as he listened to her response. "Nah, baby. There is nothing wrong. Can't I just call and tell you that I love you?"

Then he began to smile even bigger. "Alright baby, I got to go." He ended the call and sat back in his seat.

"Now that was sweet. Always tell them how much you love them because it is not a guarantee that we will make it home every day." Det. Foulks said as she smiled at him. He gave her a nod back to say, "Okay."

Thirty minutes had passed since arriving back to the station and eating lunch. A vibrant young black female uniformed officer walked into the detective division. All the male detectives stared at her. One replied. "If I were twenty years younger…"

"Don't forget you're married." Det. Foulks said. The division was filled with laughter.

"Excuse me detectives." The young officer said to them. "I think I have something you may want to see." They looked at each other and jumped up from their seats and responded in unison. "Lead the way." As they followed behind the young officer, Det. Foulks heart raced as they neared the lab. This just may be the big break we need, she thought. Upon entering the lab, the office sat at her workstation. The detective stood behind her as she typed on the computer keyboard.

"I pulled up all the footage on the intersection for Black Road and Richmond Ave as requested." They were anxious to see what she thought was key. "I went back about an hour or so before the actual time of the shooting." As she spoke the footage came up onto the screen. You can see that there is no traffic from this point, up until the time of the shooting." The officer pointed at the screen and paused the image before proceeding. "This is what I thought you should see. Here is the only vehicle that traveled on this street any time before the shooting." She continued typing on the keyboard. The image on the screen sped up to the point where Jacinta pulled up to the intersection. She glanced up at the detectives and said, "We are about to see the actual shooting. Trust and believe me, it's not pretty." The officer pressed the key to start the footage. As they watched, someone dressed in a black hoodie, approached the truck from behind. Being a mother herself, Det. Foulks was overcome with emotions as she watched the shots hit the mother and her child. Glass exploded everywhere after the first shot. They observed little Jake's five-year-old body bounce back and forth in his seat as the bullets entered his tiny frame, and as Jacinta dived on top of him.

Midway through Det. Foulks notice something and said, "Stop!" The officer and Detective Wallace peered at her. They assumed that it had been too much for her. The officer stopped the footage. "Hey, I think I saw something. Rewind." The officer did until she was told, "Stop and enhance that." Det. Foulks pointed to the hand of the shooter. The officer enlarged the image enough so Det. Foulks could satisfy her curiosity.

"What is it? What do you see?" Det. Wallace asked as he studied the screen to see what she had seen.

"Right there! Look at the wrist. That's some kinda bracelet. That's our only way of identifying the shooter." Det. Foulks said as she looked at the others. "Please continue officer."

The officer continued the footage. Once the shooter ran off, the same vehicle as earlier sped by. "Right there. That is what I wanted you to see. I've already run the plates and the vehicle is registered to a Terrica Mathis." The officer then said, "I just emailed you both the owner's information."

"We also need you to email an enhanced photo of the bracelet. Good work officer Brown." Det. Wallace said.

"Thank you, detective." The young officer said as she smiled.

"We need to get back to the hospital. Hopefully, Mr. Johnson knows this Ms. Mathis. I hope for his sake that it is not a side chick gone wild because Mrs. Johnson is going to go wild.If you know what I mean?" Det. Foulks said as she handed her partner the card from the attorneys.

"I know, right." Det. Wallace said as he took the card and made the call.

"Hello." Attorney Waithe answered. "How can I help you?" He asked.

"Hello Mr. Waithe. This is Det. Wallace. My partner and I are on our way back to the hospital. We would like to speak with Mr. Johnson. We think we may have a lead, but we need his help. We have something to show him."

"Alright, I will run it by him and see if I can secure a conference room for us to talk in."

"Thank you. We will be there shortly." The call ended.

Marcus walked back to the ICU to have a talk with Jake about the conversation he'd had. He would also check to see if he were willing to talk with the detectives. Entering the room, he noticed Jacinta and Jake arguing about Jake refusing to release JaRonda. "Excuse me. I am sorry for the interruption, but I need to speak with you, Mr. Johnson." Marcus said.

"Whatever it is, you can say it in front of Jacinta." Jake said as he stared at his son through the glass.

"Well sir, the detectives called and said that they are returning to the hospital. They would like to speak with you. They said they may have a lead to the shooter." Jacinta's eyes widen and Jake turned around to face Marcus. "What do you want to do?"

"Set it up!" Jacinta said before Jake could speak. "I will be there also." She looked at Marcus and said, "If this proves that Tone is innocent, I want to know." She looked at Jake determined. Marcus also looked at Jake. Jacinta raved, "Don't look at him. I said set it up!

"Yes ma'am." Marcus said and walked out of the room. Jake and Jacinta glared at one another. Jake was glad to know that there may be a lead, but he did not want to let Tone off the hook. He wanted a reason to make Tone hurt and feel the pain that he was feeling.

Jake walked out of the ICU and went to share the information with his family. The family felt some relief. Jake looked at Tone and shook his head in disbelief that he was still there. Jacinta came from the back also. To Jake's surprise, when Jacinta noticed Tone still there, she took him by the hand and said,

"Everything is going to be alright." Jake bit down on his lip in anger. He hated to see his wife touching the man that he despised. Witnessing her sitting beside Tone, talking, and consoling him, made Jakes's blood boil. He glared at Shanon and threw a look of disdain his way also. Although the family felt a measure of relief, they could sense tension in the air.

The detectives climbed into the car. Det. Wallace put on his seat belt and got comfortable. As he waited for Det. Foulks to turn over the engine, he checked his text messages. After a moment of doing so, he turned to her and said, "Uh, I know I'm not the smartest person in the world, but I do know you have to put the key in the ignition and turn it over for the engine to start." Then he looked at her questionably.

Det. Foulks just sat in deep thought.

"Hello…" Det. Wallace said as he waved his hand in front of his partner's face.

Det. Foulks turned and stared at him in disbelief and said, "We have to be careful of what info we give Jake. Because if he is not willing to cooperate, we may be telling him who is responsible for the attack on his family. We both know how he can make someone disappear without a trace. Their blood will be on our hands."

Det. Wallace fell back into his seat and contemplated what she said. He knew that she was correct and didn't want that to be the outcome. Then said, "You're right. I didn't think about that. So how are we going to play it?" as he stared back at her.

"Very careful. You are also right."

"About what?"

"You are not the smartest person in the world." She smiled, cranked up the engine, and pulled out of the station lot. Det. Wallace just shook his head and chucked.

# CHAPTER FIFTEEN

JaRonda could hear Mike in the kitchen as he read the text. She thought to herself that Jake must have discovered that Tone was not behind the shooting, therefore they would be forced to release her. The thoughts faded away when she contemplated the fact that little Jake had passed away. Now what would become of her and her unborn child? JaRonda started to pray that little Jake was alive and something else was going on that did not concern her.

All sorts of crazy thoughts started running through her mind once again. What would become of her daughter? Who would help raise her? Would Tone ever stop looking for her? Would he move on with his life not truly knowing what happened to her? She began crying uncontrollably.

Mike walked back into the living room and noticed JaRonda. "What's wrong with you, now? You should be all cried out. I have some good news for you." He said as he smiled at her. Her expression changed to curiosity. "Your husband and Big Tee are very brave. They are at the hospital right now trying to convince Jake that Tone had nothing to do with the shooting."

Mike smiled even bigger and shook his head. "Jake isn't buying it and told Tone that he is clueless about your whereabouts." Mike laughed and sat across from her.

"Mike, you know Tone had nothing to do with it. You just want to hurt him by harming me. If you genuinely want to hurt him, don't hide the body?" JaRonda yelled at him. "Let it be known that you killed me and his child if you are so tough. See real gangstas don't throw a rock and then hid their hand. You and Jake ain't nothing but some big cowards!" JaRonda snapped and jumped to her feet and said, "Come on Mike! You're big and bad. Kill me! Kill me, Mike! What are you waiting on?!"

"Shut up! I wish I could! Trust me, right now you're pushing it!" Mike sat up in his chair. "If little Jake don't make it, I will be more than happy to end your life." He said as he pointed his finger towards her.

As she stood looking down at him, she said, "Do you really think that Tone is going to let this go? If that baby makes it, and I pray that he does. Once he knows that you kidnapped me and held me hostage, is he going to turn a blind eye? No! He is a real gangsta and everybody is going to know that he killed each and every one of you! So, in the words of Pooh, 'I would hate to be you!" JaRonda sat back down, crossed her legs, and glared back at Mike.

Mike did not break a sweat or acknowledge in any way that he was concerned about anything. However, he knew that she was right. Tone was going to bring it and bring it hard. Whether they release her or kill her, Tone was going to be out for revenge. He already suspected that Jake was behind her disappearance. That was the reason he went to the hospital. Mike stood to his feet, pulled his gun, and walked over to JaRonda. He placed the gun against her forehead. "Ain't nobody afraid of that punk you call a husband. If he were such a so called gangsta, he wouldn't be at the hospital begging to get you back. He would have come in blasting and getting his man because that is what real gangstas do. We already know that we're not getting back the ones that have been taken."

JaRonda laughed and said, "Mike, stop it. Tone is trying to make peace. Nonetheless, once he knows that things are not going to work out, he will turn up. Now go ahead and pull the trigger. You are a dead man either way it goes." Then she pressed her head fervently into the barrel of the gun and stared Mike in the eyes.

JaRonda said, "Awww. I see you must wait until your daddy Big Jay Jay tells you what to do." She shook her head. "It's his wife and child, yet he has you doing his dirty work. You have always been his flunky. Look at you! You want to kill me but too afraid of what another man is going to think. You can't even think for yourself. Mike, go sit down! I am not afraid of your threats. You are not even in control." Mike's jaws tightened as he listened to her. JaRonda laid back in her seat. He turned and walked away. Then she exhaled in relief.

Mike paced back and forth in the kitchen in a rage. He wanted to go back into the living room and put a hole in her head. She had really gotten under his skin. He felt that he was losing control, because JaRonda was no longer afraid and was willing to die. She had called him out and there was nothing he could do about it. Jake did not want her dead unless Little Jake died. It was going to be some real drama either way. Mike started talking to himself. "Jake is tripping. She is right. We are going to be at war no matter what. Why is he waiting to kill this chick?" JaRonda could hear him talking but was unable to tell if he was on the phone or talking to himself. She realized that he was worked up and a time bomb waiting to explode. JaRonda rubbed her stomach and told her unborn child that everything was going to be alright.

Mike received a text from Shanon. "Hey fam, things are getting crazy here. The detectives are on their way back here. They said that they have something to show Jake and hopefully it will turn out to be a lead to who is behind this. I will let you know the outcome." Mike picked up a glass and threw it against the wall. JaRonda was in the other room but jumped when she heard the crashing sound.

Mike walked back into the living room. Eyes red, he looked at JaRonda and said. "They are about to show Jake the truth and then your wish will come true. I will kill you. I am about to send guys to the hospital to wait for Tone and Tee to leave. Then they will kill them. See real gangstas cover their back. Tone makes the mistake of going to the hospital. Now we know his whereabouts. Yes, in the words of Pooh. 'I really would hate to be either of you'." Mike winked and smiled. JaRonda did not say a word. All the bluff in her was gone. Deep down, she knew that

Tone was not behind the shooting, but he was a sitting duck. A hit crew was about to ambush him and Tee. They were clueless. Regardless, if the detectives' evidence could prove Tone innocent, JaRonda had allowed fear to take control again. Mike knew it.

# CHAPTER SIXTEEN

The attorneys secured a conference room and waited for the detectives to arrive. Jake sat in the ICU sulking about Jacinta conversing with Tone. "How can you sit out there and talk with that dude? You know how I feel about him. Yet you are out there all touchy feely." Jake frowned as he looked over at Jacinta.

"Stop talking to me. If you don't like it, turn his wife loose then." Jacinta shot back without looking at him. "I know you have her somewhere. Mike is the one holding her. I am not stupid, Jake. He is the only one not here and hasn't been here all day. You had better hope and pray that nothing happens to my baby." Jacinta turned and faced him and said, "I am going to make your life a living hell." She bobbed her head up and down. Jake knew that she meant every word. He just turned away and stared at his son.

A few minutes passed and the room was silent. They could hear one another breathing. Jake said, "If the detectives arrive with their information and it implicates Tone, what am I supposed to do? When my son was born, I promised him that I would always protect him. I failed him. He is laying in there and I can't do a thing to help him!" Jake hit his fist against the glass as tears rolled down his face.

Jacinta stood up from her wheelchair and walked over to Jake. She wrapped her arms around his waist and laid her head in his back and said, "Baby, you are the one that can save his life. God has put the responsibility on you. You are the one keeping little Jake from getting better. He gave you the word that he would heal our son, but you are letting your pride get in the way. If you genuinely loved us the way I know you do, you will set JaRonda free. That man came up here to prove to you that he is not the one behind the attack.

Think about. If someone wanted to get you out of the way, who better to set up than Tone? Everybody knows that you and he has been at odds for years."

Jacinta returned to her wheelchair. Jake heard every word and it had him thinking. It took a lot for Tone to come up to the hospital unarmed. Jake knew that he would have done the same thing to prove that he was innocent.

"If it is not Tone, who could it be? I hate to believe that Shanon is behind this. He really has been acting strange." Jake said aloud.

"Jake stop it. You know that Shanon would not do anything to hurt us. He knows your every move. Why would he want to hurt you or want you dead? He looks up to you and has his entire life. You are more like a brother to him than a cousin. Please get that out of your head."

"I can't think of anybody else that would try and take me out. Who would have the guts to attack my family knowing that there would be no peace in the streets until I found the person responsible?"

"Well, it is not Shanon." Jacinta said as Derek knocked on the door. "Come in."

The attorney stepped in and said, "Sorry to interrupt but the detectives are on their way up and we have the conference room ready. If you follow me, I will lead you where we will be speaking with them."

Jake pushed Jacinta in her chair and followed behind. As they proceeded through the waiting area, Jake stopped and looked at Tone and said, "I am about to find out what these cops are talking about. Afterwards, we are going to talk. I hope that you are not lying to me because if anything leads back to you, I don't know. I just don't know?" Jake eyed Tone for a moment before walking away.

As Jake walked off, Tone said. "I will be right here waiting and ready to help in any way I can."

Det. Foulks and Detective Wallace walked into the waiting area. They noticed Tone and Big Tee. They looked at each other, wondering why the men were there. It was no secret that they had been at war with Jake. Many of the city's unsolved murders stemmed from their crews killing one another. Seeing Tone and his right-hand man sitting in the waiting area, had them confused. Neither of them had spoken it, but they each suspected that Tone had been behind the attack. They hoped that they could get the matter under control before it created a war zone in the streets. Tone, Big Tee, and Shanon all shot the detectives a look of disgust.

Marcus greeted the detectives. "Hello detectives. Mr. Johnson has agreed to this meeting." He said as they shook hands. "Follow me this way. I was able to reserve a conference room. My father called in a favor. Pops know the director of the hospital." He said as they walked down the hall.

They entered the conference room. Jake and Jacinta sat on one side of the large table next to Attorney Derek. "Hello detectives." He said as he stood to shake hands. "Would you like something to drink?"

"No thank you." They said in unison and took their seats.

Det. Foulks said as she looked in Jake and Jacinta's direction. "I want to start by apologizing for my selfishness earlier. My actions were uncalled for. Please forgive me."

Jacinta smiled and said, "Apology accepted. Thank you." She looked at Jake.

"Whatever, can we get to the evidence you have for me to see?"

"Yes, but we were not expecting Mrs. Johnson to be here." Det. Foulks remarked.

"Why not?" Jacinta exclaimed.

The detectives looked at each other. "Well because some of the questions we need to ask, may be personal Jake."

"And what could that be?" Jacinta inquired as she looked at Jake inquisitively.

Jake began to breath heavily and stated. "Whatever you need to ask me you can ask in front of my wife. I don't have anything to hide."

Det. Foulks said, "Ok Jake. Do you know a female named Terrica Mathis?" She looked at Jake to observe his reaction.

Jake thought to himself for a minute. "Do you or do you not, Jake?" Asked Jacinta.

Jake looked at her and said, "No. Why would I?" He asked the detectives.

"Are you sure you don't know anyone that lives at 761 Cherrywood Lane? She drives a 2017 black Chevy Impala."

"Cherrywood Lane? That is on the far north side of town. I don't know anybody off hand that stays out there or drives a black Impala. Why what does that have to do with anything?"

"Yes, can you get to the point?" Asked Marcus.

"Hey, can you go and ask Shanon to come in here. He may know this chick because I don't." Jake said to the attorney. Derek walked out of the room to get Shanon. Moments later, shanon walked in. "Cousin, do you know a female named?" Jake paused and looked at the detectives.

"Terrica Mathis, because for some reason Jake does not know but thinks you may." Jacinta stated with attitude. Jake looked at her and shook his head.

Shanon said, "Yeah, that's Pooh's ole lady. That's the one he brought to the picnic. Why?" Shanon asked he looked around the room.

"Does she drive a black Impala?" Asked Detective Wallace.

"Yes. Why?" Shanon asked still confused. "Cuz, you do not think Pooh had anything to do with this?

He has been loyal from day one."

Jake and Jacinta eyed one another. A tear rolled down Jacinta's face. Jake looked back towards the detectives. "So, what are you saying? Do you have hard core facts to back what you are saying? That is an awfully close friend of mine. If you are not sure, don't say it. There will be conse…"

"Jake! Watch what you say." Attorney Derek said, interrupting him.

"Well, his girlfriend's car was seen on the traffic cam before the shooting." Detective Wallace was interrupted.

"Ok, what does that mean?" Shanon inquired.

"Shanon let them finish, okay?" Jacinta said. She knew that Shanon did not want to believe that anyone in their circle and close to the family could be behind the attack.

Det. Wallace continued. "After the shooting, her car was the only vehicle seen in the vicinity. Huh, just let me show you the footage, Mr. Johnson. Mrs. Johnson, you may not want to watch."

"It's okay. It has been replaying repeatedly in my mind since it happened. It is nothing that I am not thinking about right now." Jacinta stated and looked at Jake as he grabbed her hand.

"Are you sure honey?" Jacinta shook her head as to say yes.

Det. Foulks said, "You are a very strong woman." She placed a tablet on the table and started the footage. They watched and Jake dropped his head as he witnessed the event firsthand. He felt helpless and broke down in tears. His eyes widened as he watched the person run up and fire into the vehicle. He could see little Jake's body bounce back and forth from the shots. He gripped Jacinta's hand tighter as he watched her dive over to protect her child. Once the shooting was over, Jake saw that the same vehicle sped by.

Jacinta held Jake is her arms tightly as he sobbed. Shanon's forehead was pressed against the wall as he cried and hit the wall. The room was eerily quiet. Nobody said anything. The detectives and the attorneys allowed them a moment to release their pain.

Det. Foulks softly said. "Mr. Johnson, we were hoping that you know someone who wears a bracelet like this." She slid the enhanced photo over to him.

Jake wiped the tears from his eyes, picked up the photo, and stared at it. Jake jumped out of his seat hysterically. Everybody looked at him as he screamed. "NO! NO! NO!" He picked up a chair and threw it into the wall.

The detectives looked at one another. They realized that Jake knew exactly who it belonged to. They hoped that he would inform them and not take matters into his own hands. Jacinta picked up the photo. Her eyes widened and she was unable to breathe. As she grabbed her chest, tears rolled down her face, uncontrollably. Jacinta looked around the room at everyone, then said to Jake. "I.. I..I can't believe this. This must be some kind of mix up. He wouldn't … do this." Jacinta choked on her words.

Shanon asked. "Cuz, what's up?!" as he ran around the table.

"It's Mike! Man. It is Mike." Jake shouted.

"What?! Are you sure?!" Shanon asked as he took the photo out of Jacinta's hand. Shanon noticed the bracelet and let the photo fall from his hand. He stood in shock for a moment before asking Jake, "Why? Why would he do this? We are family." Shanon's knees got weak, and he fell back into a chair.

Detective Wallace asked, "How can you be so sure that it is him.?"

Jake pulled up his right sleeve and Shanon did the same. Then said. "Last year, while in New York, I bought us matching bracelets. I have black diamonds, Shanon has blue and Mike has yellow. Those yellow ones on that photo. That's how I am so sure." Jake turned his back to everyone, looked up, and yelled. "Why?! Why are You punishing me like this?!" Jacinta and Shanon turned and looked at each other. They could not believe that he was talking to God.

The detectives looked at each other with astonishment. Det. Foulks asked, "Jake would you happen to know where Mike is right now?" Her heart raced in hopes that Jake would tell Mike's location and they could arrest him before more blood was shed.

Jacinta took Jake by the hand, looked up at her husband, and said, "Do right by your son."

The detectives looked at each other wondering what she meant by that. They hoped that if that was what it takes to get Jake to give up Mike's location, it was fine with them.

Jake looked back at her then over at Shanon. Shanon remarked. "It is your call. I'm

134

down for whatever," in an angry tone. Jacinta shot him a look of disbelief. Shanon then said, "Little man is worth more than Mike, though cuz," as he stared back at Jacinta. The two detectives were still confused about what was going on but hoped that Jake would not hold back any information.

Jake shook his head at his wife in agreement and walked out of the room. Shanon followed behind. The detectives shifted in their seats as the men left the room. Det. Foulks nervously asked the attorneys, "What is he doing? Where are they going? We cannot just let them walk out of here knowing Mike's whereabouts. We will have to arrest them for withholding information. Jacinta, please try and talk some sense to your husband."

"Everything is going to be alright." Jacinta stated.

"How can you be sure? He did not say anything. They just left." Det. Foulks stood up and rushed out of the conference room. Her partner followed behind.

The attorneys and Jacinta made their way back to the waiting area where Jake and Shanon were. The detectives stood there delaying their next move. They did not know Jakes plans but knew they must not let him leave the hospital without capturing Mike or knowing his location.

Jake sat beside his mother and aunt before saying anything. They sensed that the newly revealed information was not good. Jake laid eyes on Tone, stood to his feet, and walked over to him. He said, "Don't worry about JaRonda. She is going to be fine. I am going to personally make sure of it. Just give me a minute to take care of some business and then we will go together to get her." Tone let out a sigh of relief and shook his head in agreement. Now everyone in the waiting room was curious as to what caused Jakes change of heart towards Tone, the person he once despised. Jake went over to Bishop Walker and his wife. With his head hung low, Jake said, "Bishop," then took a breath and exhaled. "It is Mike. Mike is the one who attacked my family. He personally is responsible. Mike actually shot my wife and son." Jake gazed up to face Bishop Walker. The waiting area was silent. No one said a word. Everyone was in disbelief. Jacinta was comforted by her parents. Jake's mother and aunt were taken aback by the information. Jake's mother had to be rushed to the emergency room. She collapsed from chest pains.

Mike's mother asked Jake, "Baby are you sure? Why would Mike do something like that? You two are like brothers. Are you sure about that?" Mother Walker did not want to believe that her child had caused everybody so much stress and pain. She turned to her husband with tears streaming down and said, "Honey why is Jake lying on our baby? Why would he say such a thing? Mike would never hurt Jacinta and that baby. He loves them like his own."

Bishop Walker hugged his wife and asked Jake. "Son you are sure that it is Mike?" Bishop asked in disbelief, but he knew how the streets worked. He knew that on any given day, your right hand could turn and stab you in the back. Bishop Walker turned and looked at his friend Joe who was still comforting his daughter. It hurt him to know that Mike could do this to the people he loved. He had raised him to love them as family. He glanced back at Jake as Jake said.

"Yes, sir. I am sure. I can tell by the bracelet that the shooter was wearing. There are only three of them, mine, Shanon's, and Mike's. I bought them as gifts." Jake broke down again. "I am sorry Bishop. I don't know what to do. Please, you must help me. I love Mike, but I want to kill him. I just do not know what to do. I cannot believe that he would do this to me. He's my brother. I have known him all my life. Why would he do this?"

Bishop Walker knew in his heart that Mike was truly behind it. He had to do the right thing by God. He took Jake by the hand and said, "Son, I do not have the answers that you are looking for. Nonetheless, I must be a man of God first, even in this situation that involves my son. Jake you must let God handle this. You must do what is right. Let the police know where Mike is. If you know."

Jake contemplated the Bishop's words. "Alright, but I need you, Joe, Shanon, and Tone to sit in with us when we speak with the police." Tone looked surprised but agreed as Jake watched him. "I do not want Mike hurt. I have an idea to make sure of it. Allow me to go and check on my mother first.

# Chapter Seventeen

The attorneys, detectives, and everyone Jake requested waited patiently in the conference room for him. Bishop Walker and Joe talked amongst themselves about the event that involved both of their children. Tone sat quietly and thought to himself. What was Jake up too?

A half hour later Jake and Shanon walked into the conference room. "How is Ruby?" Joe inquired.

"The doctor said she will be fine and that there is nothing we need to worry about. They are discharging her right now. They wanted to keep her overnight, but she refused. Aunt Denise and some of the other women are with her." Jake said as he and Shanon took their seats.

"Amen. God is good. I am so glad to know that Sister Ruby is fine." Bishop stated.

"Ok, Mr. Johnson. It is good to know that your mother is fine." Det. Foulks said. "But we need to know the location of Mike so that we can send a task force to arrest him."

Jake could see the anxiety on Bishop Walker's face as the detectives spoke concerning his son. "Hold up. I said I have an idea and that is why I asked Tone to be present. We are going to do this the correct way. Innocent lives are at stake." Jake exclaimed as he looked at Tone. The detectives listed and agreed to hear him out. "I had Mike kidnap Tone's wife this morning. I thought that he was behind all of this. We have to do this my way. You must allow me to handle this so that we can get JaRonda back alive." Jake could see anguish surface on Tone's face. Jake said to Tone. "Bro, don't trip. She is going to be fine as long as these two let me handle it. Mike will not make move until he hears from me or Shanon."

"Let Jake handle it." Tone insisted as he glared at the detectives.

Det. Foulks looked at her partner before speaking. "Alright. We will let you handle it, since there has not been any missing person's report filed. Technically, I cannot do anything about this. That is only if she comes out safely." She wanted to make sure Jake understood that if he kept his end of the bargain, she would also.

Bishop Walker let out a sigh of relief as Joe patted him on the back. Jake turned to Tone and said, "I am going to have Shanon call and tell Mike that my son did not make it. He will tell him that we have you and are on our way to him. Plus, we need him to call off the guys that he sent up here to wait for you and Big Tee to leave." Jake looked over at the two detectives. "Is that cool with you, Tone?"

"Anything to make sure my wife is fine. I am with it." Tone said as he nodded his head in agreement.

Jake turned to Shanon and said, "Make the call." He looked at Bishop Walker. Bishop Walker stood to his feet, nodded at Jake, and proceeded out of the room with Joe behind him.

Shanon pulled out his phone and made the call. "Hello fam. What is the word on my nephew?" Mike asked as if he were genuinely concerned. Mike had not planned on Jacinta and Little Jake being in the truck. Jake and Shanon frowned simultaneously at the sound of Mike's voice as he inquired about Little Jake.

"Fam, listen to me and listen well. Call the guys off and have them meet us at the spot." Shanon paused and said, "Little man did not make it."

"WOW!! He didn't make it?!" Mike asked as he looked at JaRonda. "How is Jay and everybody doing?"

"Fam, you know everyone is tore up. Jake and I are on our way to you. We have a guest with us. We've got Tone. We caught him and Tee slip'n. I knocked the brains out of Tee's head and grabbed Tone. Jay wants him to watch as he tortures JaRonda. Get on top of that. We will be there shortly."

"Ah…Where did it go down?" Mike asked. "Tone was at the hospital earlier, right?"

Shanon eyed Jake and the detectives then whispered. "What do you want me to say?"

Detective Wallace wrote a street name on a piece of paper and held it up.

Shanon read it and said, "Over on Larkin. Why?"

Shanon knew that Mike would send someone to check out the scene.

"Cuz, you know we had to make sure that nobody saw anything." Mike said, "If there are any witnesses, we will be able to handle it."

As Mike talked, Det. Wallace was on the phone. One of the attorneys walked back in with Big Tee. The detectives had decided to stage a false crime scene. Tone ordered Big Tee to go alone with every-thing the detectives had planned. Big Tee, along with some uniformed cops, was rushed out of the room and through the hospital, to a site to set up the false assault.

Mike looked towards JaRonda and said, "Well JaRonda, today has just gotten worse for you." He smiled and said to Shanon. "I have you on speak-er and she heard everything. You should have seen the look on her face when she heard that Tee was dead, and you all have Tone." Mike laughed and said, "I will send someone to check out the scene and be waiting." Mike ended the call. Tone's eyes were red as fire, and he was breathing heavily.

"Tone are you going to be able to hold it together? If not, I cannot allow you to jeopardize this and your wife's life," asked Det. Foulks.

Jake grabbed Tone by the shoulder. Tone jumped in defense. "Tone it is cool." Jake stated with his hands in the air. "Trust me. He isn't going to do anything to JaRonda. He thinks he has gotten away with what he has done. So, he will not do anything to ruin that."

Tone snapped back to reality. Hearing Mike's voice, taunting JaRonda, caused him to blank out. "I'm good. Let's get this done and over with, Jake." Tone glared at Jake with fury in his eyes.

"Alright Jake, where is Mike? I need to get my team there and in place before you arrive." Det. Foulks demanded. Her partner waited for the information so he could pass it on to the Task Force.

Jake took a deep breath and stared at Shanon. He knew that he had crossed the line by assisting law enforcement. The code of the streets was to never work with the law and handle business yourself. However, his son's life was on the line and Little Jake was more valuable than any street code. Shanon shook his head in agreement. "Mike is at 186 Arthur Ave." He stood to his feet and walked out of the room. Shanon and Tone followed behind. Det. Wallace forwarded the information and instructed the Task Force to stand down.

As the men entered the waiting area, Jake proceeded to Bishop Walker and hugged him tightly. His mother came to him and said, "I am so proud of you, son." She hugged and kissed him before sitting back down.

Jake turned and faced his wife and said, "Everything is going to be alright. I love you."

Jacinta smiled and spoke. "I love you more. Now go and handle your business so you can come back to me."

Jake turned to Tone and said, "Let's go and get your wife." The men walked out with the detectives in toe.

# CHAPTER EIGHTEEN

Jake, Shanon, and Tone climbed into a car. The detectives and other officers did the same. Shanon pulled out of the parking garage and into the traffic, headed to where Mike was holding JaRonda. The detectives and other officers followed behind Shanon at a distance. The three men rode in silence. Neither of them would have thought in a million years that they would be in the same space without trying to kill one another. The history between both crews had been deadly but now they were riding together. Who would have imagined?

Shanon watched Tone through the rearview mirror as Tone stared out of the window. He only imagined what could be going through his head. Tone's expression showed nothing but worry. Shanon said to him. "Tone?" Tone snapped out of the trance he was in and looked towards Shanon. "Bro don't worry, everything is going to be alright. Nothing is going to happen to your wife. She is going to be fine." Tone gave a head nod in agreement.

Jake sat back in his seat and said, "You have my word on that." He gave a small chuckle and continued talking. "Who would have ever thought that we would be at this point? The two of us, not trying to kill one another. I guess there is a God." Jake shook his head back and forth and said, "I was trying to keep my focus on you and the one that wanted me dead was right next to me." Jake's expression changed to quickly. He began to get angry all over again.

A few seconds later, Shanon said to Jake. "I just can't believe you thought it was me." He looked at Jake momentarily, then spoke. "Cuz, that hurt. I am letting you know I feel some type of way. You know I love Jacinta and little cuz. You know I would lay my life down for them both." Shanon said aggressively. Tone sat in the back seat in shock. He knew that they were like brothers and could not believe what he was hearing. However, he would never have thought that Mike would have either.

Jake remained quiet. He was already feeling guilty for even thinking that Shanon could do anything to hurt his family. He thought to himself; 'how could I think that about Shanon and never once suspect Mike.'

"So, you don't have anything to say?" Shanon asked.

Jake dropped his head and said, "fam, I am sorry. My mind was playing tricks on me. You were moving about without saying anything to me. It just seemed strange. I know you would fight a bear to save them. There isn't anything I can say but I am sorry," as he looked towards Shanon. He waited for a moment for Shanon to respond but he did not. Shanon just kept driving without saying a word.

For the next ten miles the men rode in complete silence. Everyone was wondering how things would play out. Would Jake kill Mike? (Were Shanon's thoughts) Tone wondered how he would react when he saw Mike? Jake just did not know how to react. He had too much to lose, his son's life was at stake.

The silence was broken when Tone pulled out a blunt and fired it up as they got closer to the hood. Tone took a pull then passed it to Jake. Jake hit it a few times before passing it to Shanon. The weed seemed to be what they needed to calm their nerves because neither of them knew how they would feel once face to face with Mike.

Shanon pulled into the driveway at the spot. Jake turned around to Tone and asked, "You ready?"

"Yea. Let's get this over with before I change my mind and kill that bastard." Tone said with a serious look.

"Alright, just keep your cool and follow my lead." Jake said as he threw him a towel. "Cover your head with this."

Before stepping out of the vehicle, Jake received a text from Det. Foulks letting him know that they were in position. Jake opened the back door and pulled Tone out by his arm as he held a gun to his head. Shanon noticed Pooh's girlfriend's vehicle parked across the street as he exited his.

The three men made their way to the front door of the house. Shanon used his key to open the door. They entered. Mike and Pooh sat in the kitchen talking and JaRonda sat on the couch.

Her heart stopped when she saw Jake with the gun to Tone's head. Jake walked Tone over to the couch and pushed him down beside JaRonda.

Mike and Pooh walked into the living room and started expressing how sorry they were for the loss of Little Jake.

JaRonda threw her arms around Tone's neck. He took her face in his hands and asked, "Are you okay?" She shook her head yes. JaRonda was unable to speak from crying uncontrollably. She was elated to see Tone but feared for each of them. "Baby, it's going to be okay. Everything is going to be fine." Tone whispered into her ear. JaRonda cried even harder. She knew that there was no way they were walking out of there alive. She held her husband close and cried on his shoulders.

"Baby, I know you're trying to make me feel better, but they have already dug a grave in the woods somewhere for me. Now that you're here, they're going to kill and bury us both." JaRonda paused with bulging eyes and fear on her face then spoke. "What about the baby? Where is she? Who is going to take care of her?" JaRonda started to panic! Tears flowed down even harder. She began to shake as she thought about their child.

Tone took her back in his arms, rubbed her back, and said, "Baby calm down. Everything is going to be fine. Trust me."

Mike walked up, hugged Jake and began to speak. "Bro, I am sorry about little man. He will be missed dearly." Jake bit down on his bottom lip and frowned as Mike hugged him. It took all of Jake's might not to haul off and tear Mike apart. Nevertheless, he kept his composure because he did not want to spoil the surprise.

Jake looked at Mike and said, "Fam, I am good. I got the person responsible for it. That's all that matters to me now. Trust me, he is going to pay." Then he turned and walked towards Tone and JaRonda. JaRonda grew evermore afraid, as Jake neared them. She grabbed Tone even tighter. Tone could feel the tension and fear in his wife and tried to console her.

Jake stood in front of them and stared at Tone. Suddenly, he hauled off and punched him in the face. JaRonda screamed and fell back into the couch.

"Jake please! Please! He did not do this." JaRonda pleaded for Tone. Jake just stared at her. "Please Jake. I beg you, please! He didn't do it! We have a child that go to school with your..." She hesitated and contemplated what she almost said about her child who was still alive going to school with his. "I. I. I mean. I don't know what I mean! Please Jake. I am sorry for your loss," she said between tears. "I know you're hurting but Tone would never do anything like this." She turned to her husband and spoke. "Tell him baby. Tell him you did not do it." She slowly slid back beside Tone whose lip was bleeding.

Tone looked at her and then back at Jake. "I hate, I missed and did not kill that hoe you call a wife." JaRonda's eyes widened in disbelief. "You better make sure you kill me because if you don't... I'm going to kill you, Jacinta, and that punk Shanon. I am going to make sure that I record it and send it to your mothers." JaRonda could not believe what she was hearing. The confession was more than enough, but to hear all the other things Tone said was appalling. She never imagined that he could be such a monster. In her mind, she now perceives him as being as much an animal as Jake.

Jake hit Tone again. Shanon observed the expression on Mike's face as Tone confessed to the shooting that he himself had done. Shanon frowned when he noticed the surprised look on Mike's face.

"Fam, I told you. It had to be him!" Mike yelled out as he walked over to Jake. Then he began to antagonize JaRonda. "JaRonda, what happened to Tone being this big bad gangster?" Mike laughed. "Now you will see who the real gangsters are. See real gangsters don't get caught. They put work in and get away with it. Like us. We are about to put this work in on both of you and get away with it." Mike laughed again and turned towards Tone to speak. "Tone. Tone. Tone." Mike shook his head. "You actually thought you were going to get away with coming up against us?! You tried something like this and literally believed that we were not going to uncover the truth?! You must really be crazy? Now look at you. I bet when you woke up this morning you never envisioned it to be your last one? Nigga, you have totally lost your mind. You killed my little man! He was my nephew!" Jake and Shanon breathed heavily as they listened to Mike talk about Little Jake.

Mike turned and looked at Jake. "Fam! Let me do it! Let me shoot this hoe." He uttered as he pointed his gun towards JaRonda. "So, I can watch this hoe cry!" Referring to Tone.

"Jake please?! Please don't do this! I am so sorry." JaRonda could see the intense anger in Jakes's eyes.

"Mike, give me the gun. This here is personal! I am going to do this myself. It was my son that was killed." Mike handed the gun to Jake. He smiled and winked at Tone.

Next, he asked Pooh a rhetorical question. "Pooh, what was that you said earlier? All I remember Tone, JaRonda, I would hate to be you today." Then he and Pooh laughed.

Jake stared at Tone as he held the gun. He said, "Mike, you want to hear something funny?" Jakes's eyes were red as fire.

"What's that, fam?"

"You and Pooh should not want to be you today." Mike and Pooh looked at each other. "Tone is not the one who tried to kill me or my family." Jake responded as tears rolled down his face. He turned to face Mike and pointed the gun at him. "Nigga, it was you!"

Shanon grabbed Pooh in a headlock and took his gun from his waist. He hit him over the head with the gun. Pooh laid knocked out on the floor. Mike did not say a word. JaRonda was perplexed. She looked at Tone as he grabbed her by the hand and stood to his feet. He helped her to her feet as well.

Jake turned to Tone and reached his hand out to shake Tone's. The men shook hands. "Tone, thank you for your help. Take your wife and go! She has been through enough today." Then Jake spoke to Ja-Ronda. "Mrs. JaRonda, I am sorry for everything, and I hope you can forgive me one day. I am truly sorry. Take care of my man. He loves you more than you could ever know. He is a good dude." Jake said as he looked eye to eye with Tone. "He will explain everything to you. Thanks again. I will catch up with you later." Tone nodded to Jake, took his wife in his arms, and made their way to the door. As they walked past Mike, JaRonda stopped and stared at him for a second before being pulled away by Tone.

"Come on baby. We must get out of here. I will explain everything later." Tone said as he hurried her out of the door. They were met by the Task Force agents dressed in all black and bullet proof Teflon outfits.

One of the agents asked, "Ma'am, are you alright? We have a med team waiting to take you to the hospital if need be."

"I am fine." JaRonda said through her tears. "I just want to go home and be with my daughter." She peered up at Tone.

"Sir how about you?" The agent inquired because of the blood on his shirt.

"Everything is good with me. We just want to get home to our family."

"Alright. But before you go the detectives need to speak with both of you." The agent explained as he led them to where the detectives were stationed.

"Hello, Mrs. Frankland. You don't know just how

good it is to see you alive. I am Det. Foulks and this is my partner, Det. Wallace." She stated as she reached out to shake JaRonda's hand. As they talked, an E.M.T. worker checked JaRonda's vitals. She turned and asked Tone, "What's going on in there?"

"I really can't say exactly. But if I know Jake, like I think I do, I bet he is going to kill Mike." The detectives looked at each other. "He just has that look in his eyes. Plus, Mike crossed him. His right-hand man crossed the line and attempted to kill his family." Tone said as he took JaRonda by the hand and walked away towards Big Tee.

Big Tee stood outside of his black Dodge Ram truck with the door opened. JaRonda's eyes lit up when she saw him standing there. She hugged him tightly around the neck and said, through her tears, "I thought you were dead."

Big Tee's eyes watered as he hugged her in return. He said, "Lil sis, you know better than that. I would not allow myself to die without making sure you were safe. Plus, you still owe me a chocolate cake." Tee hugged her back and said, "get in so we can get you home to start baking." They jokingly smiled at each other.

JaRonda stepped in and sat back in the seat. "Boy," she said. "That's all you think about.?" She flashed him a bright smile. "I am going to make you a triple decker."

Big Tee threw both of his hands into the air. "Yes!!" He smiled back and closed the door. Tone climbed in and they pulled off.

# CHAPTER NINETEEN

Back in the house, Jake stood in front of Mike with the gun pointed at him. All kinds of thoughts were going through Jake's mind. He thought of their childhood; how they grew up together, played video games, and stayed over each other's house. He reminisced about how they first smoked weed together and even fighting with one another. He also remembered them fighting others who dared to come against any of them. The three men were inseparable. As youngsters, if one of them were on punishment the others would help him sneak out of the house. Jake thought about the first time they all had their first sexual experience with some older girls in high school. Jake could not remember a time in his life that Shanon and Mike were not a part of it. They were there to support him when his father was killed. At the age of sixteen they helped him kill the men that were responsible for his father's death. Mike was present when Little Jake was born. That very day, he took on the title of Uncle Mike. He was the best man at Jake's and Jacinta's wedding.

"How could you do this? Why? Why would you try to kill my family?!" Jake yelled while still pointing the gun. "I love you. I thought we were brothers. I trusted you with my life! Say something! You'd better tell me something or I swear I am going to do you bad. You're going to wish that I would just shoot you in the head!"

Mike stood there a moment before speaking. He looked back at Jake and began. "I know you can care less now, but I was not intending to kill Lil man. I was not expecting them to be in the truck." Mike paused, bit down on his bottom lip, and proceeded to speak with a straight face and no regrets. "I was expecting you to be in the truck. When I walked up on the truck, lil man looked me in the face. I knew that I was not going to be able to explain it, so I shot. I shot him and Jacinta. I had to cover my tracks. I did not know that they were alive until Shanon called and told me." Mike rubbed his face. "Do what you have to do."

Jake was astonished! He could not believe what he was hearing. His hand shook as he held the gun. Mike did not blink. Jake knew that Mike was not afraid of dying. He always said that he wanted to go out like a G. Jake asked, "What is the reason you want me dead? What have I done to you?"

"I am tired of being your 'do boy'!" Mike yelled out as he pointed his finger in Jake's face.

"You tired of being my what?!" Jake yelled back waving the gun.

"Whatever you say, I do. You want someone dead; you call me, and I do it. Who did you send to snatch

JaRonda? Me!"

"That is what you like to do. You always want to put the work in!"

"Yeah, I do all that. I put the work in, I got bodies, but everyone fears and respect you. Not me!" Mike yelled and turned to Shanon. "You're not tired?! I know you should be! We do all of the work."

Shanon just shook his head and did not say anything.

"I am out here making everything happen. Not you Jake!" Mike yelled and stepped toward Jake. Shanon raised his gun to Mike.

Jake yelled back. "Respect?! Respect?! That is what this is about?! You don't think people respect you?! Nigga! We are respected because we're family. Everybody knows that we will ride and die for one another. But it is because of you that we are who we are! You did all the fighting growing up. You're the one that made everybody fear and know us. So how could you possibly feel like you're not respected, or that you are my 'do boy'? We built this together. Not me not you, not Shanon. But us! I thought you did everything you did for the family. But I guess I was wrong..." Jake cried crocodile tears as he cocked the Desert Eagle and pointed it before firing. "Bang!"

At that very moment at the hospital, Dr. Taylor rushed into Little Jake's room with an emergency team. Jake Jr. had flatlined. The beeping sound from the monitor rang out. Dr. Taylor began to do CPR as one of the nurses cut away Little Jake's gown. Another nurse set up the defibrillator. The CPR was not working. Dr. Taylor requested the defibrillator paddles.

"Turn up the voltage!" After the nurse charged the defibrillator, the doctor yelled out. "Clear!" She shocked the child with the paddles. After each try, she did another round of CPR. Dr. Taylor tried and tried. Then she yelled out, "Come on baby, fight! You must fight!" as she continued to apply CPR. Tears rolled down her face as one of the nurses grabbed her by the shoulder. Dr. Taylor dropped her head and shook it back and forth.

She lifted her head and checked the time on the clock. "The time of death is 12:55 pm," she exclaimed as she swallowed the lump in her throat. The nurse recorded the time of Jake Jr.'s death.

Jacinta screamed out, "No Lord, No! You said that everything was going to be alright. But you still took my baby away from me." She cried as she pressed herself against the glass, staring at her only child's lifeless body.

Dr. Taylor held Jacinta and tried to comfort her the best she could. Deep down inside she realized there was nothing she could do or say. "I am sorry. We tried everything that we could. His chances were slim from the beginning." Dr. Taylor stated holding back her emotions.

She led Jacinta into the room. Face covered in tears and barely breathing, she walked slowly over to Little Jake. She sat beside him, lifted him up, and cradled her baby in her arms like she did when he was an infant. Jacinta rocked back and forth, tears falling even harder. She spoke softly. "Baby, momma loves you and I am going to miss you so much. It's going to hurt." She paused as she wiped away the tears that had fallen onto his face. "Mommy is so... sorry. I was unable to protect you." Jacinta lifted her head. "Lord Jesus, I thank you for the time you have given me with my baby. Father, I understand, and I will continue to serve you with my whole heart." Jacinta looked at her child who was only five years old. She could not believe that his life was over. She reminisced about the morning and how full of life he had been. He was running through the house singing his song about the day he was going to spend with his daddy. How was life going to be now? The house would never be the same. There would be no life. Jake had not kept his word and had killed Mike. He had allowed his pride to get the best of him. Jacinta thought, 'how could he say he loves us more than anything then does something like this?'

Dr. Taylor went and informed the rest of the family about Little Jake. She also led them back into the I.C.U. so they could be with Jacinta and say their final farewells. Jacinta's parents and the rest of the family, rushed back to be with her. Bishop Walker and his wife stayed behind. They stared at one another. Sister Walker's eyes filled with tears. She walked over to her husband, wrapped her arms around his waist, laid her head against his chest, and cried. Neither of them said a word but shared the same thought. Jake had killed their son, Mike.

As Jacinta's parents made their way to her, they could hear her screaming. "Jake!!!!! Jake, you killed my baby!" She held little Jake close to her chest.

Once inside the room, her parents ran and wrapped their arms around their only child. Their hearts ached for their daughter who had lost two children in one day.

Mrs. Johnson stood in shock as she saw her grandson's dead body. She could not move or breathe. Denise took her in her arms. "Breathe, sister. You have to breathe baby." They stared at each other and knew what lay ahead. Their sons had not taken heed to the words that were given. Therefore, the curse had not been broken. If so, Little Jake would still be alive.

"Why?! Why momma? Why couldn't Jake do the right thing?" Jacinta asked.

# Chapter Twenty

Back on Arthur Avenue, Det. Foulks commanded the Task Force to "Get in position," after hearing the gun shot. The Task Force began making their way to the house.

"Jake?!" Shanon yelled out.

With gun in hand, and smoke coming from the barrel, Jake looked at his lifelong friend Mike, who had blood pouring out of him. He flashed a sinister smile at the sight of the blood. Jake had forgotten all about the promise that he had made. In his mind, Mike had to die.

Reacting to the shot, Mike grabbed his shoulder. With the look of the devil on his face, Mike turned and smiled at Jake. "Yeah, that's it. Come on, finish the job. I'm glad it's you and not an off-brand nigga trying to make a name for himself." He said as he licked the blood off his hand. "Maybe I will see you in hell or maybe not. Come on Jake! Finish Kill me! Remember, I killed Little Jake!" Mike yelled as he walked up on Jake. Jake lifted the gun and pointed it right between Mike's eyes. Jakes eyes were red as fire.

Both men appeared to be possessed. Jake licked his lips and smiled back as he prepared to pull the trigger.

Shanon yelled out again and stepped between them. "Jake?! Yes, Mike needs a bullet in the head, but Little Jay Jay needs to be given a chance at life, too. Cuz, we can break the curse. You know that I am with you one hundred percent on whatever, no questions. But this is different. We can change our family's history. Our kids could live a life without worrying about dying in the streets. Remember, if you kill Mike, you're killing your son." Shanon put his hand on the gun and pushed Jake's hand down slowly. "Give me the gun, cuz." Shanon stared into Jake's eyes and slid the gun out of his hand.

Mike stood with a look of confusion on his face. "He's not dead?" Shanon turned, faced him, and shook his head no. Mike's eyes widened as he thought about what he had done. He dropped his head and let out a sigh of relief. Seconds later, he felt a shooting pain to the face as he fell to the floor. Shanon hit Mike across the head with the gun. As Mike regained focus, he saw Shanon standing over him.

"That is the only reason you are not dead. But if he were, you would be also." Shanon said as he stepped over Mike.

Jake snapped out of his trance and looked at Mike. "Mike, I love you. Because of your actions, you have changed my life today. I know where I belong now. That is with my family. You've not only changed my life, but you saved my soul. I am done with the game. I am out. I am going to spend every moment I can with my wife and son." Then Jake looked over to Shanon. "Thanks, cuz. Thanks for making me realize what is important. I love you cuz and sorry for everything."

Shanon nodded. "I love you too, Big Cuz."

Mike and Shanon walked towards the door without looking back. They left their ex-best friend behind and walked out. Mike remained on the floor in shock that Jake had spared his life.

Once outside, the lead agent of the Task Force ran up with his weapon trained. They threw their hands up and Shanon spoke. "The guns are on my waist." The agent pulled the guns out from his waist and handed them to another agent.

"He is in there. He's alive, but Pooh is knocked out." Jake said to Det. Foulks. The agent went in to confirm that the men were alive. Once he radioed that they were alive, Det. Foulks smiled at Jake. "Go be with your family," she said. "If we need to talk to you, I will get in contact with you later." She walked past Jake and patted him on the shoulder.

Jake looked at his watch. It read one pm. He looked up at the sky and said, "Lord I kept my word. I am submitting it all to you, including my life. I am done with the game, and I ask you to forgive me for my past. Father, thank you for keeping your word and healing my son." Shanon had a huge smile on his face when Jake looked at him. "What are you smiling for?" Jake asked.

"If I knew what it would take to make you realize that God is real, I would have shot Little Jay Jay a long time ago." Shanon chuckled and smiled.

"Stop playing." Jake said before they burst out laughing.

"Get in cuz. Let's go and check out lil man. We kept our word, now let's go watch God work a miracle." They climbed into Shanon's car and drove off. As they drove off, they saw Mike and Pooh handcuffed and being placed in the back seat of one of the black SUVs.

# Chapter Twenty-One

At the exact same time that Jake submitted himself to God, Jacinta was still holding her son in her arms. Everyone there was sadden for her loss. No one could believe that the child was gone.

Suddenly they heard a voice say, "mama, don't cry. I'm here." Jacinta jumped and almost dropped Little Jake. Once she realized that the Lord had heard her cries and brought her son back, Jacinta sang praises loudly unto God. "Thank you, Jesus, thank you!"

Little Jake laid back and flashed a smile at his mother. Dr. Taylor rushed over to him. She checked the clock. It read one o'clock P.M. One of the nurses that stood beside her said, "That child was dead!" Dr. Taylor looked at her in agreement as they checked his vital signs. While the doctor and her team did their job, the I.C.U. became an official tabernacle with the family and friends praising the Lord.

Dr. Taylor stepped back from Little Jake's bed in shock and turned to his mom. "He seems to be fine. He may be in a little pain but besides that, there is no sign of anything wrong with him." With tears in her eyes, she watched Jacinta kiss her child.

Little Jake said, "Mommy?"

"Yes baby?" Jacinta smiled as she waited to hear her child's question. To her surprise, he said something that caused everyone that heard him stand still.

"I was with Jesus. My daddy kept his word, even when you all thought he didn't. Jesus said He had to show that He keeps his word and that it would never return to him void." Once Little Jake spoke those words, Bishop Walker knew that he had been with the Lord. Immediately a peace came over him.

"Yes, little man, His word cannot come back to Him void." Bishop smiled at him. He gazed up and said, "Thank you Father for saving my son's life."

Little Jake looked at his grandma Ruby and smiled. "What else did Jesus say?" She asked as she smiled at him with tears streaming down her face.

"He said that He is going to use my dad and Uncle Shanon in a very powerful way. He said you would never have to worry at night about receiving a phone call saying they were hurt." His grandma was flabbergasted! She knew that she had never uttered words of worry about Jake or Shanon in his presence. She smiled, nodded, sat in her chair, and cried.

A half hour passed. Shanon pulled into the parking lot of the hospital. The sun was shining immensely as they made their way to the entrance. Shanon and Jack felt as if the burdens of the world had been lifted from their shoulders, but both were too elated to speak.

Once they entered the elevator, Jake heard the music again, "For My Good but for God's Glory," by LaShun Pace. Jake seemed to be the only one to hear the music. Shanon was talking but all Jake could hear was the lyrics to the song.

The doors opened to the third floor, they stepped out laughing and talking, as they make their way to the I.C.U. waiting area. The waiting area was empty. Jake and Shanon looked at each other. They joy quickly turned into fear. They hurried down the hallway to Little Jake's room. As they approached, they could see the room filled with people, many of them crying. They became nervous as they stood frozen, staring through the window.

Jake's mother noticed them. She walked over to Jacinta and whispered in her ear. "Hey, look who's back." Jake and Shanon entered the room. Everyone departed from beside Little Jake's bed.

When Jake saw his beloved son lying there with a huge smile, he rushed over to him and wrapped his arms around him. Little Jake let out a sigh from the pain. Jake laid him back down, turned, and hugged Jacinta.

"Daddy, I missed you."

Jacinta stepped back and looked at everyone in the room. "Ain't that something! The only one he missed is his daddy." The room filled with laughter.

Jake wiped tears from his eyes and said, "I missed you too, son."

"I was shot three times. I'm a G now, like you." Little Jake declared as he looked at his dad. Jake was speechless. His wife and mother looked at him to see how he would respond. Jake just dropped his head. Little Jake said, "Dad you said that you were a G when you got shot and that Gs don't die. I didn't die, so that makes me a G too." Jake remained silent. Tears rolled down his face. He knew that he had been teaching his son the wrong things and today things had to change. As Jake lifted his head and looked at his son, Little Jake said, "Daddy don't cry. It's too many people in here. They may think you're soft." Everybody in the room broke out in laugher.

Jake spoke to his son. "Baby boy, being shot does not make you a G. I was wrong. Doing what is right is what makes you a G. It is okay for a man to cry when he is happy and overjoyed about someone he loves. I am crying tears of joy because I love you." Jake bent down to give his son a kiss. Little Jake reached out his arms and hugged his dad. There wasn't a dry eye in the room.

"I love you too, dad."

# Chapter Twenty-Two

Three years later, September 7, 2023 a beautiful Sunday morning, the sanctuary of Faithful and Holiness Apostolic Church was filled to capacity. The church was in its praise and worship hour. After forty-five minutes, Bishop Walker signaled for the choir and congregation to settle down and get ready for the next part of the service.

Bishop Walker walked up to the pulpit and said to the congregation, "Praise the Lord, church!" The congregation responded with a loud cheer. "Hallelujah!" They didn't just stop there with shouting back God's praise; they gave the creator the highest praise.

Bishop Walker was dressed in an all-white robe which represented a special occasion. He was going to announce to the congregation the individual that would become his new assistant pastor.

"Amen Bishop Walker! This is the day that the Lord has made, and we are going to rejoice and be glad in it," yelled Jacinta's father.

"Today is an incredibly special day for the church. We will receive a new assistant pastor." Bishop Walker turned around and gestured for Jake to come out.

"Please help me welcome our new assistant pastor, Pastor Jake L. Johnson with a hand clap and praise."

The whole congregation stood to their feet in ovation. Pastor Jake walked over to Bishop Walker and hugged him before proceeding to the pulpit. Assistant Pastor Jake stood and stared out at the audience. He saw his family and friends staring back at him. His mother, Auntie Denise, and Mother Walker were just a few women that were on the Mother's Board.

Tone and JaRonda were there also with their two daughters, Ke'Andra and Kiemirrian. Big Tee, Donnesha, Shanon's wife and their newborn baby shared the same pew with them. Following the turmoil with Little Jake, Shanon and Dr. Taylor began dating and were now married.

Ex-detective Foulks, her husband and family were seated in the back with ex-partner Wallace and his family. They all came out to support Jake on this special day. The Waithe family had also joined the church. Jake was elated when he noticed one of his cousins there.

Pastor Jake walked down from the pulpit and stood in front of the congregation momentarily collecting his thoughts before speaking. Overjoyed, he turned and faced the alter, raised his hands, and began to praise God.

"Heavenly Father, I stand before you today to say that if it had not been for the Lord on my side, I know emphatically that I would be in a grave or locked up for the rest of my life. Lord, because of your mercy, I can stand here and praise your name. Heavenly Father I want to thank You for loving us so much that You gave your only begotten son to die on the cross so that we may have life more abundantly.

Jesus, I give You glory for what you have done in our lives. Because of You, who were wounded for our transgressions, bruised for our iniquities; the chastisement of our peace was upon him... By your stripes, my son is healed."

The church was in an uproar. The spirit of the Lord had fallen on the members. They were shouting and praising God all over the church for what he had done and brought them from.

Once the praises to the Most High had settled, Pastor Jake made his way back to the pulpit. He opened his bible and prepared to give his sermon. The subject of his message was about breaking the generational curse.

"If you will, turn with me in your bibles to Deuteronomy, chapter 28. We will read verse fifteen, then jump down to verse eighteen. That will be our focal point for the day. Let's go to the Lord in prayer."

Pastor Jake prayed. He asked the Lord to anoint him to be able to deliver the message that He had given him for his people. "Verse fifteen. It reads as follows." 'As he began to read, the spirit fell upon him and anointed his words. "But if you do not obey the voice of your Lord, being faithful to do all his commandments and his statues which I command you this day; that all these curses shall come upon you and overtake you...' Let's jump down to verse 18. This is where I want you to really pay attention. It reads as follow; 'Curse shall be the fruit of your body.' Let's stop there for a moment.

The word fruit here is representing your children. The Lord is letting you know that a curse shall fall upon our children simply by disobeying his word. Proverbs 26 says, 'Like a flitting sparrow, like a flying swallow, so a curse without a cause shall not alight.' Here the Father is telling us that a curse will come because of something that we did, by disobeying his orders. It's not just by happenstance, there must be a reason." Pastor Jake took the microphone in his hands and began to walk around the pulpit.

"Church, I want to share a story with you. This very subject is something I learned about three years ago. I was under a generational curse." He held nothing back. He told them everything. He even went into how he had kidnapped JaRonda. His mother and auntie could not restrain from crying.

Pastor Jake went on to tell how his grandfather and father had allowed their pride to get the best of them. They refused to take heed to warnings that were given to them by the men of God. He spoke on how he was doing the same thing, but Shanon reminded him of what he would loss if he did not heed to the word.

"The pastor of the church that had officiated my grandmother's funeral had given my grandfather a word from God. He was to let the Lord handle it. He wanted to, but because my father was so young when he found his mother that way, it interfered with my grandfather's thinking. He felt obligated and refused to walk away.

My grandfather found each one of the men responsible for my grandmother's death and killed them all. The whole town knew what he had done. The pastor told my grandfather that he had brought a generational curse on his family."

Pastor Jake looked at his mother and auntie, knowing that he and Shanon had caused them much pain also. "When my grandfather moved his family up here from the south, my father met two guys that would end up being tighter than brothers to him. They grew up and went to the streets together. They became notorious on the streets and money was no issue for them. The two men that I am referring to are Bishop Walker and Joe Cole, my father-in-law. Bishop Walker and Deacon Joe Cole had their hands up in the air praising God for their deliverance.

"The night that my father was murdered, he had gotten a word from God. There was a situation that had arisen involving a large sum of cash that was missing. Bishop Walker told my father that God said to walk away from it. If he chose not to, his wife and sister would suffer dearly. My father had told Deacon Cole that he was going to take heed to the warning he had received. Deacon Cole fell back. That is why he is still here with us today."

Deacon Cole, his wife, and Jacinta shouted out, "Thank you Jesus!"

Unfortunately, my father..." Pastor Jake began to cry softly.

"Take you time son," Bishop and Mother Walker told him.

"...he had too much pride and he could not just walk away. My father was killed that night."

Jacinta was standing and crying as Pastor Jake spoke his peace. She knew he had been crazy about his dad, just like Little Jake was about him.

"My father did not obey God and that curse that his father caused, was handed down to him, and on to Shanon and me. My grandfather was a hustler, my father was a hustler, and Shanon and I were hustler. We picked up where my father left off. Not because of necessity, but that was a part of the generational curse. Every man in our family was to become hustlers, and in turn, every woman in our lives would suffer tremendously."

When my wife and son were shot, all I could think of was killing someone, anyone that had something to do with it. My son had only a thirty percent chance of living. In my mind, someone was going to hurt just lie I was hurting." Tone put his arm around JaRonda, who was crying as she re-lived that awful day in her mind.

"But by the grace of God, Bishop Walker spoke to me. He explained that God wanted me to let it all go. Remember, the curse was on me. I had that same pride as my father and grandfather. To make things worse, Shanon was going to go all the way with me. This time it was going to be my mother, my auntie, and my wife that would suffer. We were going to lose Little Jake. I know for a fact that Shanon and I were going to die in those streets." Pastor Jake walked down from the pulpit and stood on the ground level in front of the congregation.

"Hallelujah! Church, I am here to tell you all that if you obey the word of God, he will fulfill his promises to you." Pastor Jake motioned for Little Jake to come forward. Little Jake climbed down from his seat next to Ke'Andra.

"God's word tells us in Hebrews chapter twelve verse one: 'lay aside every weight and the sin that so easily entangles us...' NIV version. Those are the sins that we commit like live so openly in fornication. The word of God says, 'Don't even let it be named once among you.' This is in Ephesians 5:3. 'We're not to hold any hatred in our hearts or malice,' Ephesians 4:31. Mark 11:25 says 'To be forgiving because God has forgiven you.'"

Little Jake was up front with his father by this time. The church was standing on their feet and clapping their hands. Loud shouts of 'thank you Jesus' and 'hallelujah' came from different sections of the congregation. Pastor Jake bent over and picked up his son, all the while speaking God's word.

"To break the curse, do as Romans 12:2 says, 'present your body as a living sacrifice, holy acceptable unto God.' How do you do this? By not being conformed to this world and being transformed by the renewing of your mind. Also, by getting into your word, praying, and meditating daily. This is found in Joshua chapter one verse eight.

I John 2:15 tells us that we are not to love the things of this world. Church, today is the day that I recommend each person to break the curse on their life." The Spirit had fallen over the masses from the power of the Holy Ghost.

"Malachi 3:9 tells us that we are cursed when we don't pay our tithes and offerings. Church. The Lord said that if you do not want the curses of Deuteronomy 28:15-68 to come upon your children and your children's children, you need to turn from your way of living. Believe me, I know!

In the book of Isaiah 55:10-11," as Jake began to exegete the scripture, several of his family and friends stood to their feet. "God said that his word was like rain and the snow that had come down from heaven. So shall my word be that goeth forth out of my mouth: it shall not return unto me void, but it shall accomplish that which I please and it shall prosper in the things where to I sent it.

You see, what the devil meant for bad, the Lord meant for good." Pastor Jake hugged his son then said to the church, "God said that if I walked away from everything and just let him handle it, my son would be healed. As you can see, he is healed. Hallelujah! Thank you, Jesus!!!" Pastor Jake fell to his knees with his son in his arms.

Bishop Walker called for Jacinta to come up to the microphone. She handed her three-month-old child to JaRonda, then proceeded to the microphone. Music started in the background, and she began to sing:

I've been through the storm.
I had mountains in my life.
But through it all, I learned to trust in Christ.

He made a way out.
When I stepped out on faith.

That's when I began to see the sunshine
though the storm.
Now that I am free. I love to praise His name.

Oh, Jesus I love to praise your name.
Oh, Jesus I love to praise your name.
Oh, Jesus I love to praise your name for
all your goodness you give.

The Lord took me with all my faults.
He didn't hold my past against me.
He cleaned me up and dressed me in
righteousness.

Oh, Jesus I love to praise your name.
Oh, Jesus I love to praise your name.
Oh, Jesus I love to praise your name for
all your goodness you give.

Jesus took me the way I was.
He placed His love around me.
Can't explain the way I feel,
But I can go on and on about the love
Jesus gives.

Pastor Jake's cousins had also walked from the back
and gave him hugs because they too were once under the curse. Jacinta walked down when his cousins
walked down to the altar and placed her arms around
her husband and son. She said, "Thank you for saving our family." Pastor Jake began to cry even harder.

Little Jake said, Mommy, can I now work the job that my daddy works?"

Jacinta smiled, "Yes you may."

The choir was singing. Over one hundred and fifty people received the Holy Ghost that day.

# PREVIEW OF SOULMATE

## Soulmate: Chapter One

Derek: Hello, Sister Gayle. How are you? Welcome, come on in and make yourself comfortable. Shania will join us in a moment. While we wait, may I get you anything? Something to drink or eat? You name it and it is done. [Derek and Gayle hug one another.]

Gayle: Thank you sir. A glass of water will be fine. And thank you for allowing my crew and me to invade your life with this interview. I know you and your wife have terribly busy schedules. [Gayle took a seat across from Dereke]

Dereke: Not a problem. Plus, this isn't the first interview you've done on me. [Dereke poured Water into a glass]

Gayle: Yes, you are right, but this is a very special one. [seconds later, walks in Shania]

Shania: Hello, hello. I am sorry for keeping you waiting. How are you? Please forgive me. [Big smiles. Shania hugs Gayle then kisses Dereke and sits back down beside him.]

Gayle: Aww... I just love seeing Black Love. Ma'am it's not a problem. I know that you are really busy.

Dereke: Alright. Since we are all here, how can we help you Sister Gayle?

Gayle: How about sharing how you two met? [Gayle flashed a big smile.]

Dereke: [Dereke and Shania turned and faced each other and laughed] Well, that's a story and then some. From our first encounter, I would not have thought we would be here together.

Shania: Yes, that was a day that I will never forget. I don't think we ever shared that story with anyone. You will be the first.

Gayle: Well do tell. I bet it was like a fairytale, a love story. [Dereke and Shania laughed.]

Dereke: Far from it. [Laughed and took Shania's hand]

Shania: Watch it! [Smiled]

Dereke: Well Sister Gayle, this is the story of how I stole Shania's heart.

Shania: What?! You stole my heart? It's the other way around. I stole his. [Smiled and laid her head on

Dereke's shoulder.]

Gayle: Well, he must have done something because I can see stars in your eyes every time you look at him. I can also see them in his eyes. Every time I see you two together, you remind me of the Obama's. They look at each other the same way. Look at you, smiling with your head on his shoulder.

Dereke: Gayle don't pay her any attention. I am the one telling the story. [Glanced at Shania and smiled.]

Shania: Make sure you tell it right then.

Dereke: Gayle, as I was saying, it was on February 22, 2023, a Friday evening.

Gayle: Wow! You remember all that? Most men don't remember anything. I'm sorry, continue.

Shania: He remembers everything but what he is supposed to. [The room filled with laughter.]

Dereke: Once you hear the whole story, you will know why I remember. And yes, it was a Friday evening. I had flown into Atlanta, GA. I was met by Jake and Shanon, whom you know are my cousins. We had business to attend to there. I stepped off the plane and there they stood. I couldn't do anything but shake my head. Jake had a big smile on his face and Shanon appeared to be mad at the world.

Then Jake yelled out, "What's up cuz?!"

I responded back with, "Nothing, but what's up with you?" Then we hugged.

I then asked Shanon, "What's your problem? Why do you look like you're mad at the world?"

Shanon responded in an aggressive tone. "It's cool out here!"

I stepped back and looked him up and down.

I said, "I don't know how you're so cold. You have a bear on."

Shanon said, "Nah fam, this here is chinchilla. Don't get it twisted."

"Well excuse me." I replied before turning my attention back onto Jake. They both had full length minks on standing in front of a white Rolls Royce SUV. The SUV was owned by Jake and he had a white coat to match. Shanon had a black coat on. He is a big man, standing six feet plus.

Then I said. "I guess somethings will never change."

Jake flashed that million-dollar smile of his and said, "What are you talk'n about, cuz?" He knew exactly what I was talk'n about.

In response to him, I said, "Really? You two standing there in full length minks. My fault, Chinchilla's." I cut my eyes in Shanon's direction when I corrected myself. I followed up with, "To Top It Off, you are in front of a $300,000 dollar Rolls."

Jake being Jake had to correct me and stated, with his arms spread wide, "Um, cuz this here cost four hundred thousand."

I laughed and said, "Whatever. If we get pulled over in this and it's very possible being three black men in America, they are going to swear that we're moving weight."

Gayle: It's a shame to have to think like that, but it's true when you are black in America. Plus, a black man.

Dereke: Yes, Gayle it is a shame. You can make your money the right way, but in the eyes of some, you're still a criminal. And that is why I said what I said.

But Jake came back with, "We will throw out hands up and yell out. Black Lives Matter!" Really loud, hands in the air.

Then Shanon said, "Jake, listen who's talk'n. He just stepped off a private jet that's his own." I looked over my shoulder at the jet and didn't have a comeback. When someone's right, I can't argue with them.

But I did say, "That doesn't change the fact that you two are standing here look'n like drug dealers." Shanon, said, "Don't hate the swagger."

Gayle: [LOL!] You guys are crazy.

Dereke: That's just the half of what happened. Let me tell you what they did to get a good laugh out of me.

Gayle: Please, do tell. [soft laugh]

Derek:  Shanon said, "Explain to me how you forgot your strap and you know that we were here to handle business?" I told him I was rushing.

He replied, "Whatever. Well I copped you a new fo-five and a halter." Then Shanon opened the back door to the SUV, said, "It's in the case on the back-seat." I peered inside and there was a gun case. I quickly peered back at them. They laughed, and we climbed into the SUV.

Gayle: What?! No, they didn't? Are you serious?

Dereke: [Laugh] Yeah. They stayed on joke time. But let me explain before someone gets the wrong idea. We met in Atlanta for a national meeting for the Faithful and Holiness Apostolic Association. I had forgotten my bible. So, I texted Shanon to ask him to buy a new one for me. That was my first mistake. By doing that I set myself up for a prank. Inside the case was the bible and leather carrying case. Let me make that plain first. But as you know, my family members and I were street guys. So, we still used street terms for certain things. As guys that stay strapped with a gun, we would call our bibles, our strap. I know it sounds crazy. [Laugh]

Shania: The craziest thing, I have ever heard. [Laugh]

Gayle: Me, too! [Smiling]

Dereke: Hey, we couldn't help it. But anyway, when Shanon said he brought me a fo-five, which is the street name for a forty-five-caliber pistol, he was referring to the Holy Bible. Four letters spell out Holy and five letters spell out Bible.

Gayle: All..... OK, I get it. [Smile]

Shania: Just crazy. But he still doesn't leave home with out it. [Laugh]

Dereke: They thought it was funny because I'm a felon. I didn't think it was, but I have to say it was creative. [Laugh] Now that was just the first part of that evening. The crazy part of that evening was when we reached the Hilton Downtown Atlanta.

Gayle: Why are you hiding your face ma'am? {Smiling]

Shania: [Shake her head and smile at Dereke]

Dereke: Because she... well, let me just tell you. I walked through the lobby returning some texts and wasn't paying attention. That caused me to bump into this female.

Shania: Female?! [Face twisted]

Dereke: That's what I said. I bumped into this woman. I looked up to say excuse me and that I was sorry. But the woman cut into me and said, "Excuse you! You need to watch where you're going." Then she rolled her eyes, walked off, and then said, "Drug dealers get on my nerves. They think they rule the world. Going to end up in prison and it serves them right." I turned to Jake and Shanon who were laughing.

Shania: You heard her say all that? [Smiling]

Dereke: Did I. [As he smiled back] While laughing hysterically, Shanon said, "Cuz, you were right. Somethings will never change, like your luck with women. You still know how to make them snap and chase them off." I looked back at the woman as we made our way to the elevator. She was still furious. I said to myself, "I would hate to be the man, that has to deal with that angry black woman, if she even had one."

Shania: Why she has to be an angry black woman? You bumped into her. [with a side eye and smiled]

Gayle: Wait a minute. Were you the woman?

Shania: Who was the angry black woman, Dereke? [Smiling]

Dereke: Gayle, you're going to get me in trouble. [Laughing]

Shania: You're going to get yourself in trouble. [Smiling]

Gayle: Whoa!

------------------------

## *Chapter Two*

Dereke: Moving on Gayle. I was scheduled to preach that night and boy was I nervous. This was my first time attending a national meeting. To be the one to start it off, had me shook.

Gayle: But why? You are an awesome preacher.

Dereke: Thanks, but there were so many men of God in there that I looked up to. I guess that's why.

Gayle: Well, you are awesome.

Shania: Yes, you are bae. [Kiss Dereke on the cheek]

Dereke: Bishop Walker walked over to the podium to announce me. And I tell you, he brought the house down is an understatement.

Bishop started off by saying, "Praise the Lord!" And in response "Hallelujah!" Roared back from the thousands of saints that filled the Georgia Dome. He went on to say, "Amen. It is my privilege to introduce to you an incredibly special, young and single brother, I must add." Women shouted out all kinds of things.

Shania: UH! [Side eyed Dereke]

Gayle: You're digging yourself a deeper hole. [Laughing]

Dereke: Continuing, Bishop said, "He has a testimony that will bless you and change your life. God has truly blessed him. He was ordained into the ministry by our beloved Bishop Jackson. Since his passing, he has taken the position as head Pastor of the Faithful and Holiness Church in the Southern District of Illinois." There were many members from our home base church there. They shouted out, "Amen! That's my pastor, he's talking about." I can't lie. It made me feel proud to be their pastor. It says a lot when the members love you the way they loved the one before you. A lot of the new members were in the streets like I was. Then there are those that knew how my family and I used to run the streets of Mt. Vernon. They knew about our past criminal activities. Now to see that we had become new men in Christ, they were proud of our change.

Gayle: Amen!

Dereke: Amen, is right. They really know that I am for real about my mission. There is a brother in our church that told me one day. "He said, "I knew that I could be saved when I saw how your life had changed."

Gayle: Wow! Really?

Dereke: Yes, Bishop then said, "Well as you can see from the response, he has to be doing a good job. I know for a fact that he is because there are still great and wonderful works of God still happening in their church. That reminds me of II Kings chapter 2:9. Elijah asked Elisha, "What may I do for you before I am taken from you?" Elisha replied, "Please let a double portion of your spirit be upon me." Church that is what's going on there. When Bishop G.E. Jackson passed away, God placed the same spirit upon this brother. The lame walk, the blind has sight, and the deaf can hear. The power of God is still working there." By that time, the dome was in an uproar. Saints were shouting because many had been healed and delivered from some kind of stronghold. The musician had it rock'n. It felt like a Sunday morning worship service. Bishop Walker let it go on for a while, then he signaled for the musician to calm down. He continued with "Amen, Amen! Everybody, please stand to your feet and help me welcome Pastor Dereke D. Cartwright!" Thousands of saints stood, shouted, and clapped. If you weren't aware that there was a convention, you would have thought there was a sporting event going on. I stood to my feet. I turned to my cousin Jake and we hugged. I also did the same with the other Bishops and ministers before

I walked over to Bishop Walker, who waited by the podium for me. We embraced. I thanked him for that wonderful introduction. Then I replaced him in front of the podium. I nodded my head at Shanon who sat beside his wife Dr. Latanya Taylor-Johnson. Shanon nodded back and smiled. Before I spoke, I gazed at the saints that filled the dome. My heart was filled with joy as I looked upon the many different races that formed that sea. I said, "Amen! That was the intro. It was heart felt. I had to remember who he was talking about because I just knew it couldn't have been me." I laughed and so did everyone else. "His Introduction turned into praise and worship. How do I follow that?" We all laughed again.

"Brothers and sisters, we have a phrase we say at our church before we start each service. If you will, repeat after me; if it had not been for the Lord who was on our side, where would we be? Think about that for a minute. As you do, let me tell you where I would be. I would be dead and in hell. How can I say that? Because I know how I lived my life, and it wasn't in line with God's word. But God had a different plan for my life. God saved my soul by allowing me to go to a federal prison. Yes, you heard me correctly. I said prison." There was a man there that yelled out, "me too".

I said, "Amen brother." Then continued with, "Bishop Walker said I have a testimony. I want to share a little of it with you. God gave me a promise in 2002. I stood on that promise when it didn't seem like it was going to come to pass. In 2003, I was sentenced to four hundred and twenty months to federal prison. I was charged with conspiracy to distribute large sums of kilos of crack and powder cocaine. But what Satan meant for bad, the Lord turned and used it for my good. Prison saved my soul."

"Before we get into the word God has for us to-night, I often think about my cousin. That Is Pastor Jake, for those of you who don't know. God saved his soul in a different way. I don't think I would have been able to handle what he was faced with." I looked at Jake and he smiled at me. Then I made eye contact with Jacinta. She also smiled back, giving me the okay to share about that awful event."

Pastor Jake's first sermon was about breaking a curse. Even though we are family, he and Shanon were brought under a curse by their grandfather. My grandmother and their grandfather were sister and brother. But the men from her bloodline and I were under a different curse that came upon us by her. The curse upon us was that all the first-born male would end up in prison. And we did. I said prison saved my soul. But Pastor Jake had a different path he had to take. His wife and only child were shot one morning. Sister Jacinta's situation wasn't as severe as their son. Their son had only a thirty percent chance of living. To top it off, someone awfully close to Pastor Jake was behind the shooting. Back then Pastor Jake wasn't someone that you crossed and got away with. God spoke to him through Bishop, to let it go. If so, He would bring Little Jake out, without any compli-cations. Pastor Jake was a man, full of pride so when the actual shooter was revealed, it brought Jake to a crossroad. He had to decide if he would be controlled by pride or the love he had for his son. I had to go to prison, but Pastor Jake's family had to pay the cost for God to get his attention. As you can see, he submitted to God. God showed up and showed out. The doctor said one thing, but as we know, God has the final say." I glanced at Dr. Taylor Johnson who had been Little Jake's doctor. She witnessed the power of God when He brought Little Jake back from death. She submitted to God and joined the church. Now she testified about what she saw, and it has caused her to be a witness to her colleagues.

The dome was back in an uproar. The bishops and the ministers were shouting. Jake, JaRonda, Tone, and everybody that had witnessed the power of God that day, were praising God. Once again, I had to signal for the musicians to calm the music. "Amen, Amen! God is Good. Turn to the book of Hebrews, chapter 10, verses 35-36." As the saints went to the passages, I prayed and asked God to anoint my words, that those under the sound of my voice may receive the word and apply it to their lives. "I had a conversation with the man of God that came up under as a child. That was Bishop Allen. I went to see him and talk with him when I realized that the feds were look'n for me. Before I could say anything, God had already told him. Bishop told me everything that would happen to me even before I would get caught. He told me that they would go by my house, my moms, and then put me on the news. They did exactly that. He also told me that I would receive a lot of time. And I did. But he also told me that they would have to take it back. As you can see, they did. If you recall, I stated earlier that I stood on the Promise that God gave me. By me growing up in Greater Bible Way Church in Joliet, I saw Bishop speak things to people and it all came to pass. So, my confidence was in that promise. I also had to do something and that was go through the storm, learn how to be obedient, and submit my life to God. Once I did, God moved the mountain out of my life. I used to speak to the mountain and say; I believe what was spoken to me by the angel of God. I believe God and that it shall be even as it was told me. And in due season, God brought the promise to pass and brought me out of prison without me doing all that time. May I say one thing, but God always has the last word. When it didn't look like things were going to happen, I had to remember what God had said and had already done. I stood my ground on God's word and the devil and his demons relented in their opposition and the answer came. Amen, let's go to the word and see what God has for us.

Verse 35 reads as this; Therefore, do not cast away your confidence, which has great rewards. Verse 36; For you have need of endurance, so that after you have done the will of God, you may receive the promise.

Brothers and sisters, we are not to let anything cause us to cast away our confidence. No matter how it may look. If we know God said it, we must hold on to it. We must get into the word, read the promise/

promises and meditate on them. Speak it out loud because faith comes by hearing and hearing by to word of God. This is how we keep our confidence. Confidence is our assurance of certainty that what we ask, we will receive. The same way you had confidence in that seat when you sat down. You did not think twice before you flopped down. And that is the same way you are to be when it comes to your faith in God. Amen?!

God told Abraham in Genesis Chapter 17:5; I have made you the father of many nations. Abraham had no children and Sarah was barren. But God said Abraham was already the father of many nations. If God said it, it is true even if you don't see it in the natural. God can't lie. God calls things which are not as though they were. According to Romans Chapter 4:17-25; Abraham's human reason for hope being gone, hoped in faith that he should become the father of many nations as promised. Get the promises in your spirit and call things which are not as though they were. The more you do and see God move, your faith will shoot sky high. In the natural things don't look like it was going to happen for Abraham. And things don't look like they will happen in your life. But as children of God, we do not look at the natural, but the unseen. I had to be like Abraham. When laws were changed, I would file and get denied. I had to remember God gave me a promise. I had to stop looking at the natural and keep my focus on God. I had to keep speaking. I believe what was said to me. God told me, through another great man of faith, to pack my stuff and prepare to leave. He said act as if it is happening that day. I was obedient and did what was told to me. God kept his word and that is why I stand before you today.

What God has done for me, he will also do for you. Once we submit to Him, live according to His word and stand on His promises. Nothing and I mean nothing will be able to stand in our way. God brought Pastor Jake through his tribulations when he became obedient. He brought me through mine. God is not a respecter of persons. Therefore, I know He will bring whomever through theirs. Look your problem in the face and tell it, your confidence and faith are in God! Amen!"

The dome was back in an uproar. Saints were all over shouting and praising God. I turned the service back over to Bishop Walker and then got my praise on.

------------------------

## *Chapter Three*

Gayle: That sounds like it was a wonderful night. Wish I could have been there. Now I want to go back to something that you said earlier.

Dereke: What's that?

Gayle: Ma'am, you called them drug dealers? [Wide eyes and smiling]

Shania: [Dropped her head and laughed] Yes, if you could have seen them and their cocky behavior. You would have thought the same thing. But in my defense, they were ex- dealers. So.

Dereke: So, nothing. Like I said, being black in America, you will be judged if you have any money. [Smiled and stared at Shania]

Gayle: He makes a good point there, ma'am.

Shania: Hey! Whose side are you on?

Gayle: My apologies. Team women. [Gayle, hands up, then room filled with laughter]

Shania: That was a night to remember. The spirit moved through the dome. People received the spirit of God. Those that were sick, were healed. What I really remember about that night was Bishop Walker laying hands on a woman and said, "I am going to pray for you according to Mark 16:17-18 that God heals you of this stomach cancer." He prayed and the woman started vomiting. She vomited the tumor up.

Gayle: Whoa! I really wish I had been there.

Shania: I had never experienced anything like that in my life either. Now the most memorable part of that night for me was when Dereke walked up to the podium. Gayle, my mouth dropped. I could not believe my eyes. He was the drug dealer, so I thought, who had bumped into me earlier. I felt sooo bad for being so rude. I had treated the man of God bad. I know you're not supposed to treat people that way.

Gayle: So, you were the angry black woman?

Shania: [Puts hands on head and shake it up and down] I was so ashamed.

Dereke: Serves you right. [They faced each other and laughed]

Shania: I'm sorry baby. Give me a kiss.

Dereke: Nope. Not going to pull that one on me now. Everybody is going to know how bad you treated me. [Then smiled}

Shania: Remember that later when you try to kiss me.

Gayle: Mmmm [Smiled]

Shania: Where was I? All Yeah. Dereke, Jake, Shanon, and some more brothers were talking. I slid up behind and bumped him kind of hard. He turned around and started to speak. When he noticed it was me, the look on his face was priceless. You would have thought he saw a ghost. I said, "You again?!" Girl I put my hand on my hip and shifted my weight to one side. He just stood there.

Gayle: [Laugh] No you didn't do him like that? [Then looked at Dereke]

Shania: Girl, yes. I had to break the ice some way. So why not the way we started. He backed up, threw his hands up and said, "I am so sorry. I am also sorry for earlier. Please forgive me?" I peered over his shoulder and Jake and Shanon were waving their hands and shaking their heads to say no. I could not do him like that.

So, I said, "No, please forgive me for my rudeness earlier. I was having a bad day. That is not an excuse for being rude. So, will you all accept my apology?"

Jake and Shanon said no problem, all is forgiven. Then Shanon said, "Dereke has that effect on all women. Don't you cuz?"

He patted him on the shoulder. Then he and Jake laughed and excused themselves.

I said to this one, "How about you?" I smiled and waited.

He proceeds to say, "I'll have to think about it." Then laughed.

Dereke: I should not have forgiven you.

Shania: Whatever. I introduced myself.

"My name is Shania Guerra." I extended my hand. I went on to say, "Your message was awesome. It really was what I needed to hear. It inspired me to stop focusing on the natural and keep my attention on my prayer and confidence in what I prayed for."

Gayle: What did you think about that? Her telling you how much your message meant to her.

Dereke: [Smiled, glanced at Shania] To tell you the truth, I didn't hear anything she was saying for a moment. I was captivated by her beauty. She was the most beautiful woman I had ever been that close to. Her mocha brown colored skin blended flawlessly with the long straight jet-black hair, highlighted with brown streaks. She wore it parted in the center which caused some fine strands to flow over some areas of her face. Long curls rested atop of her shoulders. [Dereke wiped a tear from Shania's face as she listened] The way she wore it seemed to naturally display her perfectly pieced together African American, Indian, and Italian features. I couldn't help but stare into her sparkling hazel eyes, despite the slight tint on the Chanel eyeglasses. Shania was beautiful to me. I always had a thing for a woman that had nice curves, bowlegs, and pigeon toed. I don't know why, call me strange. But she was all that. [Smiled] She covered her curvaceous figure with a green and brown turtleneck sweater, a green suede skirt and a green quarter length suede coat. She also wore a pair of green crocodile knee high boots. Next, I said, "God are you sure?"

Gayle: You asked that, Why? [Looked confused]

Dereke: [Smiled] Because God spoke to me that she was my soulmate.

Gayle: Wow! Isn't that something? By being a man of faith, why did you question God?

Dereke: Because of what I experienced from her earlier that day. I just knew she was crazy. [Laughed}

Shania: Yeah, crazy for falling for you. {Smiled}

Gayle: That is so sweet. Why can't all me be like that? They are not built like you…Ma'am you hit the jack pot. [Hold hand over her heart]

Shania: He's alright. [Smiled and looked at Dereke] Plus, he was delighted the Lord said I was his soulmate.

Dereke: What I was, was afraid of you.

Shania: You can say whatever makes you feel good. You see him smiling. I stole his heart that night. He told me he was pleased that I was touched his message. He couldn't have been too afraid. He said all that while continuing to hold my hand.

Gayle: Really? She had you hypnotized. You go ma'am. [High five and laughed]

Dereke: Moving on. [Smiled]

Shania: He asked if I was visiting Atlanta. I told him no, I live there and am a member of Bishop Smith's church. I sit on the board that's in charge of the national meetings, when held in Atlanta. Then He told me, "Oh, is that so. Bishop Smith has invited me many times, to come and preach at his church."

I in return asked, "What's been stopping you?"

Before he could respond, my daughter LaShontae interrupted us. She came to tell me that she was going to ride with my parents. They were going to go out for dinner with some of the members of the church. They would drop her off later. I told her that before you do anything, you need to introduce yourself to Pastor Cartwright. She did and said that his message was good. They shook hands. She turned back to kiss me on my cheek and whispered in my ear, "He's cute." Then walked away.

I shook my head. He smiled because he overheard her. Then said, "She's cute, how old is she?"

I said, "fourteen, but thinks she's twenty-one."

We laughed about that and he said "I know what you mean. One of my sons just turned sixteen and you can't tell him anything. I just shake my head at him sometimes. Here he comes now."

Marcus came to tell his dad that they were going to go out to eat and that his paternal grandma, would like to know if he wanted to come along. If not, would he like for them to bring him something back.

Dereke: Gayle I was hungry, but I didn't know if or when I would see her again. So, I told Mark I would ride with Jake or Shanon to grab something one the way.

Gayle: Yeah, you were hypnotized. [Laughed]

Shania: But he was right about that Marcus. He introduced us. Mark spoke. I messed around and said, "Marcus, you are a very handsome young man. I bet you have all the little ladies fighting over you?"

Gayle, the boy smiled at me and said, "Thanks for the compliment. Not all the ladies, just a few." Then he smiled.

I laughed and said, "I know he didn't," as I looked at his dad. I told him, "Boy, you are a mess. Well go right ahead then with your bad self." He thanked me again then walked away.

He is still the same. I find myself laughing sometimes when I look at him and think back on that night.

Dereke said, "I told you. He is like that all of the time." I couldn't say anything. Then he said, "Wait until you meet the rest."

I asked him, "So, there's going to be another time that I'll see you again, huh?"

He responded, "If you allow it." I told him I'll have to think about it then smiled. We had small talk about things that I don't remember. Then I asked him, "Um, if you would like, I could give you a ride to your hotel. That is if it's ok and not a problem. Don't want any members jumping to conclusions. Plus, it's on my way home," which wasn't totally true. I just wasn't ready to leave his presence.

He agreed, then went and told Jake. When he returned, we made our way through the crowd. I thought about a prayer that I'd prayed a few months before. I asked God to send me a God fearing, good looking, and family man. However, we had our challenges and had to keep our confidence in our prayers. [Stared at one another]

Gayle: Nothing comes easy, but I am so glad you two kept your faith.

# Afterword

I hope that you have enjoyed the story. I also hope that it has helped you to think about where the Lord Jesus Christ has brought you from. Don't ever lose hope. Put your faith and trust in the Lord. Turn from the way you are living your life and allow GOD to order your steps. Psalms 37:23. The word declares that those who put their faith in the Lord, are blessed. He shall be like a tree planted by the water that spreads its roots by the river, and it shall not see fear when heat comes, but its leaves shall be green. It shall not be anxious and full of care in the year of drought, nor shall it cease yielding fruit. Jeremiah 17:7-8. (Amplified Bible)

The word is saying that no matter what comes we will be taken care of. All you must do is cry out to the Lord with an open heart. He is ready to receive you. The Lord declares that he will give us rest if we come to him. Matthew 11:28-30. Follow your heart. Break your generational curse!!!

# ABOUT THE AUTHOR

**DEREK WAITHE** was born to Alan B. Waithe and Jenneal (Todd-Waithe) Whiteside on December 24, 1972. When he was a child, his mother moved from Mt. Vernon, IL to Joliet, IL where he was raised. Derek graduated in 1991 from Joliet Township High School West Campus.

He says, "My mother did her best to raise my two brothers and me. She brought us up in the apostolic faith at Greater Bible Way Apostolic Temple. My beloved pastor was Bishop Samuel Allen, Sr., whom I miss dearly.

Even though I was raised in the church, it did not detour me from ending up in this prison cell where I am writing this book. My family members and I were charged with a drug conspiracy. Our conspiracy began in 1997 and ended in 2002 with me.

The family was known in southern IL as the "Royal Family". The name seemed to cause us more pain than happiness. The "Royal Family" started off as the name of the rap group that my younger family members went by. With us being so close, people just started calling us "Royal Family". They would say 'there goes one of those Royal Family boys.' Then the younger cousins added "CT", meaning "Cutthroat". That made matters worse. It went from being a group name to an organized crime family that supposedly had ties to the "Gangster Disciples", if you let the feds tell it.

The family was feared by some, hated by many, and loved by a few. The name caused so much pain. Because of it, we ended up with lengthy sentences. I was given 420 months (35) years."

# SAY THEIR NAME!

| | |
|---|---|
| Tony Mc Dade | Jemel Roberson |
| Mya Hall | Arron Bailey |
| Christian Taylor | Calin Roguemore |
| Keith Childress Jr. | Shelly Frey |
| Cariann D. Hithon | Natasha McKenna |
| Aura Rosser | DeJuan Guillory |
| Maurice S. Gordon | Samuel DuBose |
| Janet Wilson | Miguel Espinal |
| Alton Sterling | Tony Robinson |
| Jerame C. Reid | Antwon Rose, Jr. |
| John Crawford III | Dontae Hamilton |
| Stephon Clark | Michael Brown |
| Yvette Smith | Willie Tillman |
| Bettie Jones | Phillip White |
| Jamar Clark | Ezelle Ford |
| Mikel McIntyre | Malissa Williams |
| Manuel Ellis | Ronell Foster |
| Keith Lamont Scott | Akiel Denkins |
| Miles Hall | Freddie Gray, Jr. |
| Terence Crutcher | Michelle Cusseaux |
| Pamela Turner | Shantel Davis |
| Paul O'Neal | Shereese Francis |
| La'Vante Trevon Biggs | Rumain Brisbon |
| Mirian Carey | |

# WHERE IS THE JUSTICE?

## J. Kenkade PUBLISHING®

*Our Motto*
*"Transforming Life Stories"*

# Also Available from
# J. Kenkade Publishing

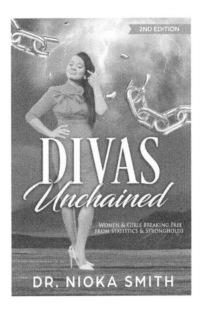

ISBN: 978-1-944486-25-9
Visit www.drniokasmith.com
Author: Dr. Nioka Smith

Sexually abused by her father at the age of 14, pregnant at the age of 17, and a nervous breakdown at the age of 28, Dr. Nioka Smith's painful past almost killed her, until the voice of the Lord guided her into destroying strongholds and reversing Satan's plan for her life. DIVAS Unchained is the powerful chain-breaking reality of the many unfortunate strongholds our women and girls face. Dr. Nioka uses her divine gift to help women and girls break free from destructive life cycles and prosper in all areas of life. Satan has lied to you. It's time to expose his lies. It's time to break free!

# Also Available from
# J. Kenkade Publishing

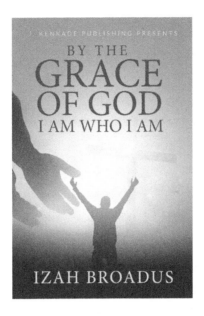

ISBN: 978-1-944486-58-7
Visit www.amazon.com
Author: Izah Broadus

Having seen death and having experienced multiple near-death occurrences himself, the author sets out to admonish and encourage others about a life that Christ gives that no street life can provide. After constantly watching so many young people and adults lose their lives to the streets and giving up on Jesus Christ, The Holy Spirit inspired the author to write this book to encourage others that there is hope in Jesus. From the streets to the pulpit, Izah helps others understand that the same God that helped him out of his lost situation is that same God that loves them as well.

# Also Available from J. Kenkade Publishing

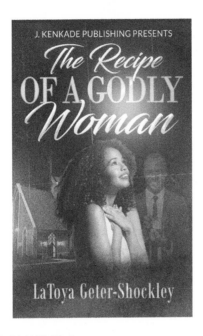

ISBN: 978-1-944486-70-4
Visit www.amazon.com
Author: LaToya Geter-Shockley

A single pastor moves to a segregated town to lead a church deeply rooted in sin. Without knowledge of the sin, he begins to casually date the church clerk. While attempting to bring both sides of the town together, he meets a single mother filled with anger, betrayal, hurt and secrets and finds himself losing sight of God's direction for him. A life-threatening storm destroys the church and the town but opens his heart and leads him to the true woman of God.

# Also Available from
# J. Kenkade Publishing

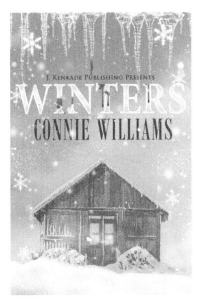

ISBN: 978-1-944486-40-2
Visit www.amazon.com
Author: Connie Williams

Winters is a captivating and passionate Christian suspense novel about a powerful, spiritual family who is anointed and ordained by God Almighty. You will feel love, pain, heartaches, compassion, grace, mercy, suffering, and God's spirit, all in one story. Find out why Winters is about the coldest season of the year in more ways than one. Come and live in the minds and hearts of Stella, Abe, Mr. Perkins, The Langley family, Hattie, Benjamin, and Minnie. So much more awaits you in this powerful Christian suspense novel. Both fiction and nonfiction, Winters will give you a chill like never before.

Made in the USA
Monee, IL
23 February 2022

91686118R00132